ADAM'S ARK

AND

THE GREAT PANDEMIC

A PLAY

By

ED STRUM

REMDUST PUBLISHING
Adam's Ark, Copyright © 2024 by E C Strum
All Rights Reserved
ISBN 979-8-9852109-0-3

Dedicated to Ernest Pugh

May You Forever Be In Our Hearts and Minds

<u>Acknowledgements</u>

I wish to extend my appreciation to Tom Steers for his technical consultation in the early stages of development of the radio play and his subsequent comments and suggestions.

Many thanks also to Leslie Brown, Heather Couthaud, Jim Hooper, Jim Jacobs, Sandra Geist and Brad Strum for their review, comments and suggestions about the play.

I also wish to extend my appreciation to Ernest Pugh for his review, support and comments concerning this play, and to Eric Concord for his review and insightful and challenging comments as well.

Thanks also to the reading group of Eric Concord, Cathie and Craig Nett, and Lisa Moretti. Hearing it read out loud was extremely helpful in improving dialogue and imagery.

Books by Ed Strum

THE CONNOISSSEURS – A Play

MONTOBA: THE PRINCESS OF ÉLEVÉ – A Novel

THE BURROW – A Play

JOURNEY OF THE SCROLLS – A Novel

JOURNEY OF THE SCROLLS – SPECIAL EDITION

THE PRINCESS OF ÉLEVÉ – A Play

EVERY DAY IS A GOOD DAY – A Play

THE HOLLOW PENCIL – A Play

CASCADIA and THE GREAT PANDEMIC – A Novel

ADAM'S ARK & THE GREAT PANDEMIC – A Play

RICHIE – A Poetic Play in One Scene

A SENSORY FEAST – An Anthology of Prose Poetry

INTRODUCTION

The genesis of this play began decades ago with the fear of nuclear war, and subsequently various kinds of chemical warfare such as that used in the Vietnam war, which continue to affect people to this day. However, it became clear long ago that biological weapons would eventually become the means of mass warfare (and mass destruction).

DNA and other scientific evidence indicate that mankind reached the brink of extinction seventy-five thousand years ago. If mankind again reaches near extinction, it likely would be the result of biological warfare or a natural cataclysmic event, rather than via nuclear or chemical warfare. The pandemics of the Black Death of 1347, the Spanish flu of 1918, and the coronavirus, are not known to be of biological warfare origin. This play was initially written before the current pandemic, and represents the hypothetical result of massive biological warfare. Coronavirus shows the extensive impact one single everyday virus can have on worldwide civilization.

A play that has a multi-racial cast featuring characters of different racial heritages, which might be the natural result of a Great Pandemic, and my visits to Tristan da Cunha, where racial diversity is the result of naturally occurring events, have solidified my desire to write such a play. Adam's Ark combines these two themes.

Four survivors of the Great Pandemic, all seeking a safe haven in a world of desolation and lawlessness, come together in the confines of a barn, a burrow, which provides a place of shelter, safety, sustenance and survival, and a focus of fertility. They are joined by two others, fleeing a dying community. This ethnically diverse group consists of:

- A writer, well-educated, yearning for home and security.
- A survivalist, well-educated, resourceful, streetwise, dreamer, visionary, yet practical.
- A vagabond, streetwise, uneducated, resourceful, earthy, yearning for a mate, with a strong desire for nurturing.
- A revolutionary, self-sufficient, idealistic.
- Two young "warrior women", sharpshooting champions.

They have their own individual goals, roles, and desires, and coexist with feelings of isolation, hopelessness, and helplessness. When threatened from outside, they come together to confront the dangers. As their inevitable launching into the outside world approaches, they prepare to leave as a team with common goals and plans. The underlying goodness of man slowly emerges, and the characters are filled with joy, hope, love and humor.

ADAM'S ARK

AND

THE GREAT PANDEMIC

ADAM'S ARK and THE GREAT PANDEMIC

CAST OF CHARACTERS (4M, 4W)
(In order of appearance)

Grace – Older than Che (see App. D) – Black heritage
Adam – Older than Grace (see App. D) – Mixed Ethnicity
Shu ("Sly"), W – Early twenties (see App. D) – Asian heritage
"Che", M – A little older than Sly (see App. D) – Hispanic heritage
Voices (Off), Stranger
Sarah – Late teens (see Appendix D) – Any ethnicity or race
Sam (W) – Late teens (see Appendix D) – Any ethnicity or race
Harry – A little older than Sarah
Ben – A little older than Sam
Note: The Stranger can be played (off) keeping cast size at eight.

Background: The play takes place in 2034, in a hay barn near a river that flows into an ocean. The ocean is to the west of the barn and the river flows east to west. The barn is on the north bank. The entrance faces west and slightly north toward the location of the habitat of the farmers, some miles away. The land is open grassland, and slopes down toward the river. The front of the barn sits higher than the back. The river bank has tall grass and reeds and the back of the barn is not far from the banks of the river.

ACT ONE
Scene One: End of fall as winter approaches.
Scene Two: A few minutes later.
ACT TWO
Scene One: Over a month later.
Scene Two: Two days later.
ENTR'ACTE
ACT THREE

Running Time: 90 to 120 minutes
Sound effects and lighting are absolutely essential to the play.
Appendix A: Author's Notes to Director and Actors
Appendix B: Set Design Considerations
Appendix C: Prop and Sound Comments
Appendix D: Comments on Characters, Humor and Costumes
Appendix E: Directing and Acting in the Round

SET

The scene is the lower section of the back of a hay barn, which has two levels in the back half. Normally this barn contains hay as well as equipment but, in this case, it was completely filled with hay bales in the fall. The real entrance to the barn is implied offstage above. A room has been created in a corner of this lower section, against the back of the barn, with hay on all sides stacked to the floor above separating the upper section from the lower. Entrance to this hay room is via a step tunnel that comes from high in the barn. The implication upon entry is of sliding down the tunnel and then crawling in from the tunnel in the hay.

One side of the room faces the back of the barn and is implied to be one bale thick so that a bale can be removed to allow smoke out, air in, and to listen. In the center of the room against the back of the barn the floor boards have been removed to create a deep dirt pit for a fire. The fire pit is circular and surrounded by large boulders to protect the barn and hay from fire. A large old grate spans the top of the pit. This fire pit is only used at night when the smoke cannot be seen. There are two old rough logs to sit on, one on each side of the fire pit. An eventual exit is uncovered in the floor. This escape hatch is covered by a bale of hay. The overall feeling is of a claustrophobic burrow.

A small (unseen) side room has been carved out on one side. The main room contains backpacks with attached bedrolls, camping equipment that one takes on a backpack trip. Everything is very old. It is late in the day, nearly dark. The dim light through the slats in the back of the barn is augmented by one or more candles sitting near the fire pit. It feels like an underground burrow or bunker.

In creating the set (see Appendix B: Set Design Considerations), care must be taken in keeping the directions of the outside environment consistent with dialogue, sound effects and lighting. The river is to the south side of the room, the back wall through which light comes and smoke goes is to the east and the entrance above is on the upper west side of the barn. Activity with strangers via sound effects and voices is also generally above and to the west end. The audience looks through an invisible wall of hay bales and no activity occurs with this solid wall of hay.

If the play is staged in the round (Appendices B and E) or thrust configurations (see Appendix B), the use of sound effects creates the illusion that the audience is inside the intimate space of the barn with sound effects and lighting behind the seated audience.

And God saw that the wickedness of man was great in the earth. The earth also was corrupt before God, and the earth was filled with violence.

And the Lord said, I will destroy man whom I have created from the face of the earth; both man, and beast, and the creeping thing, and the fowls of the air; for it repenteth me that I have made them.

But Noah found grace in the eyes of the Lord. (The Lord said) But with thee will I establish my covenant; and thou shalt come into the ark, thou, and thy (family). And of every living thing of all flesh, two of every sort shalt thou bring into the ark, to keep them alive with thee; they shall be male and female. And take thou unto thee of all food that is eaten, and thou shalt gather it to thee; and it shall be for food for thee, and for them.

And God blessed Noah and his (family) and said unto them, Be fruitful, and multiply, and replenish the earth.

Genesis, Chapter VI, IX.

ADAM'S ARK and THE GREAT PANDEMIC

ACT ONE

Scene One*: A woman enters from the side room. She shuffles in on straw covering the wooden floor. She takes a large pot from behind a hay bale, picks up a gallon wineskin, pours some water into the pot and puts the pot on the grate. She takes onions and leeks from a burlap sack, and puts them near the pot for use in making a stew.*

She is wearing very old, worn clothes, shirt and pants, as a transient hobo might wear. These clothes and those of the other characters were once of very high quality, expensive when purchased. She reaches into her backpack and pulls out a set of old rolled up papers and a pencil. She unrolls the paper, thinks for a moment, sits near the candle, and begins writing on one of the sheets of paper.

SFX*: (B/G) Soft muffled sound of rushing water nearby as a river rushing downstream, mixed with sound of wind racing across the open grassland, rustling reeds near river. There's a loud thump (outside above off). Silence. She grabs a shotgun from behind a hay bale and cocks it.*

GRACE
Who's there? That you, Adam? Who's coming down? Speak!

Adam enters. He wears overalls and a checkered jacket. He drags a large burlap bag.

ADAM
Don't point that thing at me. It might be loaded.

GRACE
It is. Two shells.

ADAM
My God, you coulda killed me.

GRACE
Why didn't you answer?

ADAM

Didn't hear anything. That tunnel's getting smaller. Too many twists and turns.

GRACE

Did you cover the entrance? With a hay bale?

ADAM

Course I did.

GRACE

See anyone out there? Still some light.

ADAM

Not a soul. Wild and desolate. Nature's taking back the land.

GRACE

What about her? Did you see her?

ADAM

Nope.

He takes out a few potatoes and parsnips and puts them near the other vegetables. He looks at her and back to the pot. He drops the sack and goes into the side room. She sits down and starts writing.

GRACE

What're you doing?

He doesn't respond. She looks at the pot then returns to her writing. He returns without the jacket, looks at the pot and then at her. She finally stops writing for a moment.

ADAM

Why didn't you start the fire? It'll take a long time for this stew.

GRACE

Someone'll see the smoke. Whatta ya have in the sack? Potatoes? And what are those?

ADAM

Parsnips. Beets and turnips too. *(Puts them out.)* Harvested mosta the potatoes. I'll hide the extra.

GRACE

Where? *(No answer.)* If you leave them behind, they'll find them.

ADAM

I found a small shed up along the river. Overgrown with reeds and grass.

GRACE

Hope you can use the leeks and onions next to the pot. *(Long pause.)* How long 'til we'll have to move on?

ADAM

A couple of weeks. Winter's here. The farmers are using lots of hay now. They'll discover the tunnel soon.

GRACE

Can't say I'll mind too much. It's stuffy here. I feel claustrophobic. Can hardly breathe.

ADAM

Thought you liked it here. It's like a home now. It's spacious.

GRACE

Hay all round us. Hay above us. Sleeping in that little room all surrounded with hay. Like animals in a burrow, underground, waiting to be dug out. Like rats in a hay barn. I feel as if I'm breathing hay. I even find hay in our food. I want a home with fresh air and a view.

The lighting has been gradually dimming as they talk.

ADAM

Think I'll try the radio. It'll be dark soon.

SFX. Radio crackling and whistling as he runs through frequencies.

GRACE

It's no use. There are never any transmissions.

ADAM

There could be someone left, trying to transmit on some frequency.

GRACE

It's a waste of time.

ADAM

Must be someone out there besides the farmers.

GRACE

Where'd you learn about this radio stuff?

ADAM

I'd left my farm to join a group of four others on a forty-four-foot Nordland sailing trawler to fish. I was the navigator and operated the ship's radio too. When some of us saw that this monstrous pandemic was deadly and spreading fast, we tried to go far from it, out to sea.

GRACE

That was a good idea. Where'd you go?

ADAM

Headed for the southern oceans. Antarctica. It was summer. Stopped at ports for food and water but saw the pandemic was everywhere. Only a few people here and there, all very sick. We left quickly.

GRACE

I'm not surprised. What'd you do?

ADAM

Tried to stay at sea. We rounded the Horn, stopped at the Falklands.

GRACE

That's a long journey. Any signs of life there?

ADAM

None. We went ashore to find water and food but left in a hurry.

GRACE

And then what did you do?

ADAM

Went to South Georgia, and stopped at Grytviken.

GRACE

Does anyone live there now?

ADAM

Yes, and they were still alive. A couple named Pam and Oliver. They were unaware of global danger and wondered why they hadn't seen any ships for months. We explained what we had seen and heard. It was a year from the time we'd left and winter had arrived in the South. When we first arrived, Jose and Kiran showed signs of illness. We quarantined them in case it was one of the virulent viruses. It was too late. They faded quickly, grew weaker, and died within a few days of each other. We buried them in the cemetery near Shackleton's grave.

GRACE

Must have been sad. What did you do then?

ADAM

We stayed several months with their blessing. We waited out the snowstorms and heavy winds until spring arrived in the southern hemisphere.

GRACE

Where'd you go then?

ADAM

Headed for Tristan. I've been there before. We had high seas and heavy winds and it took three weeks but we made it into their small harbor. They greeted us with cheers, and a member of the Glass family, Herbert, recognized me. However, we couldn't go ashore. They were turning away all ships and people to be safe.

GRACE

Now, that's smart. Then what?

ADAM

Herbert told me that only one ship had arrived in the past year and the crew of the ship had told them harrowing stories of the pandemic in Africa and Europe. Thousands of people perished in an awful manner. Some just gasped for breath and collapsed. Others lost control of all parts of the body until they just stopped moving. The worst thing reported by the ship was the body being covered with a flesh-eating bacteria that caused them to scream in excruciating pain. Some were just put out of their misery.

GRACE

That's horrible. No wonder they don't want anyone to come ashore.

ADAM

I told them what I'd seen on our journey and then asked if any of them would like to join us on our return trip. We needed two able bodied seamen, and would return the way we'd come, fishing in the Southern Ocean on the way to the Pacific. We told the Chief Islander named James Glass we'd seek a place in the Pacific to wait out the end of the pandemic, and would return the two Tristanians when it was safe.

GRACE

I'll bet they didn't go for it.

ADAM

The Tristanians declined and said they were sorry: everyone was needed to survive since they'd lost all of their trading connections. It was as if they'd gone back in time two hundred years.

GRACE

You can't blame them. So, what did you do then?

ADAM

I asked if we could trade some of our salt and spices for water and a small amount of meat to augment the fish we caught as we sailed. The Chief Islander said they could spare water since they had lots of it, and they could also spare meat from their cattle.

GRACE

That was kind of them. Then you left?

ADAM

The Tristanians wished us well, and we headed for the Falklands.

GRACE

What will they do? The Tristanians have no way to sail away.

ADAM

They'll survive.

GRACE

What about food? How will they survive without ships arriving?

ADAM

They're amazing people. They have lots of water from the volcano mountain, lots of cows on the other side of the mountain, they grow all sorts of vegetables, and they fish in the sea. They ration salt and spices. It's true they can't go far in their long boats. They're isolated and have depended upon visiting ships. I wish them well. They are a hardy, healthy multi-ethnic community.

They stop talking for some time and then Grace continues.

GRACE

Then you left the Falklands and made it back around the Horn?

ADAM

It was tough but we made it all the way to the Galapagos with Al, Bart and me. Then Al and Bart died. I sailed solo back to the river.

SFX. Sound of radio as he continues trying frequencies.

GRACE

You're wasting your time. Nobody's gonna answer.

SFX. Radio turned off. He stirs fire, chops kindling on log with axe.

ADAM

I'll get the fire ready to go. Be dark soon.

GRACE

Before they discover the entrance, can't we fill it in? Move it lower?

ADAM

They'll see the bales were broken. Gotta be gone before they do.

She shuffles sheets of paper around trying to organize her notes.

ADAM

What're you doing?

GRACE

Writing! My journal, can't you see?

ADAM

You making the stew?

GRACE

(Snappy) I started it! You can finish. I'm busy now.

ADAM

I grow all the food – why can't you make the stew?

GRACE

You think this isn't important?

ADAM

More important than eatin'?

GRACE

This is my job, to record what happened.

ADAM

What're you talking about?

GRACE

Herodotus, Tacitus, Plutarch and Pliny.

ADAM

Who are they?

GRACE

Ancient Greek and Roman historians.

ADAM

Well? So what. They're not gonna help us eat.

GRACE

If it weren't for them, we wouldn't know much about their history.

ADAM

Someone's gotta make the stew. *(He's stymied, cuts up vegetables for the pot.)*

GRACE

I'm up to the pandemic now. You can help. When did it start?

ADAM

It's been going on for five years, but it started long before that.

GRACE

What do you mean?

ADAM

This world was filled with corruption, violence, greed, and racism back then. It was growing, sanctioned, and applauded from highest levels. Mobs were growing, bigotry was rampant, guns were carried everywhere. Honesty and decency were under siege.

GRACE

(Quietly.) I know all about racism. It's part of a much bigger issue.

ADAM

What do you mean by that? What issue?

GRACE

It's called discrimination. If it isn't about black people like me, it will be about Chinese or Japanese or gays or another tribe.

ADAM

Or Jews. I understand. Many people will always find a way.

GRACE

(She nods.) Back to the pandemic. Who started it?

ADAM

Them, not it. It's greater than one pandemic.

GRACE

What?

ADAM

There's more than one deadly virus. Everywhere we went, stopped for food or fuel, they described it differently. Spread by touching, sneezing, wind-blown. Some caught it from food, or animals.

GRACE

How do you know there was more than one type of flu?

ADAM

Symptoms were different but all lethal. Coughing, spitting blood, in the brain. Just went crazy. For some, they couldn't keep food down, like a deadly stomach flu. Starved to death. There were even signs of the flesh-eating bacteria. Sometimes people just stopped breathing.

GRACE

That's what the Tristanians heard. How do they spread so quickly?

ADAM

They were designed to. Most of the time people got some type of virus before they even had symptoms, after it had already spread.

GRACE

Who started all these virus types? All at the same time? Crazy.

ADAM

This was planned on a massive scale, not an accident.

GRACE

But who? Who could it be that did it?

ADAM

Could've been anyone. Even us. But many countries have such labs.

GRACE

All these countries couldn't work together. They hate each other.

ADAM

Sabotage. That could be coordinated. Why're you asking me all this?

GRACE

(Snappy.) You're old enough to remember how it began!

ADAM

You were old enough. We survived. That's what matters.

GRACE

(Sharp.) We never talk about it. We hardly talk about anything!

ADAM

I work from dawn to dusk, trying to survive. What's to talk about?

He chops up vegetables into pot. She shuffles paper as she writes.

ADAM

Wonder if anyone's out there. *(He continues still agitated.)*

GRACE

Pull the hay away and look.

He pulls hay bale from wall and looks out. Dim lighting by this time.

ADAM

It's getting dark. Better start the fire.

SFX. The wind gets stronger. He uses candle and paper to start fire.
SFX. There is a faint scratching noise coming from the back wall.

GRACE

(Long pause.) Why're you so nervous?

ADAM

Thought I heard something.

GRACE

Who'd be around here? It's nighttime.

ADAM

I wish I could see outside. I'm sure they can hear us.

GRACE

They're far from here. Don't worry. *(She writes.)*

SFX. The scratching noise is louder and shakes several boards.

ADAM

I heard it again. I'm sure of it. It's coming from the back.

He peers through the slats in the back of the barn and shrinks back.

ADAM

It's a cougar trying to get in. She must smell the stew.

He grabs shotgun, runs to tunnel, and scrambles up to outside.

GRACE

Leave her alone. She's just hungry.
SFX. Sound of shotgun. He returns quickly.

GRACE

You didn't shoot her, did you? She did no harm.

ADAM

No, she ran away. But then I saw two people far away down river.

GRACE

How could you see them that far away? They'd hear the shotgun.

ADAM

Good eyes. The wind'll muffle the sound. But I'd better be careful.

GRACE

Not much we can do about them – if it was anyone.

ADAM

Maybe you're right. My imagination.

She starts to write while he paces on straw on wood floor.

GRACE

Tell me more about how it could've begun.

ADAM

I don't know, but when this started five years ago, the rumors said there were explosions in secret biological labs all around the world.

GRACE

Explosions? In more than one lab?

ADAM

All about the same time. Fires or explosions. Strange.

GRACE

How could that happen? It doesn't make sense.

ADAM

Sabotage. I told you before. Think I'll try the radio again.

SFX. Radio crackling and whistling as he runs through frequencies.

ADAM

Nothing.

GRACE

Those old batteries won't last if you keep trying.

ADAM

I only try at night. I've backup batteries.

GRACE

Who are you trying to reach?

ADAM

Must be some out there besides these farmers. Some good people.

GRACE

Maybe there is and they'd be worried too. Why only at night?

ADAM

Signals travel better then. Ionosphere's lower.

SFX. Radio noises. He turns it off.

GRACE

What's that? *(No answer. He goes to tunnel.)* Where're you going?

ADAM

Up through the tunnel. I hear something. Those people must be back.

GRACE

It's your imagination.

ADAM

This time, I'm sure. Where're the night binoculars?

GRACE

Over there. *(She points. He gets binoculars.)*

ADAM

I'll be right back. *(He goes into tunnel.)*

GRACE

Be careful! *(She adds vegetables, returns to write. He rushes in.)*

ADAM

Someone on horseback's coming toward the barn. Douse the light.

She kills the candle. Hoof beats closer, circling the barn and leaving.

GRACE

They didn't stop. Must be a patrol. They must've heard the shotgun.

ADAM

Maybe. I've got to be more careful. They must be getting suspicious.

GRACE

He didn't stop so he wasn't too suspicious.

ADAM

I also saw another one in the distance. At least a mile away.

GRACE

It's dark. How could you see that far? Must be a tree.

ADAM

Wasn't a tree. Not with four feet.

GRACE

Think there's more?

ADAM

Maybe. I think they're gone. No sign of her. Don't think he saw her.

GRACE

She'll be back. She's a night animal.

ADAM

She's like a feral cat. A survivor. Streetwise.

GRACE

Must be a few survivors. Somewhere.

ADAM

Yeh, but mosta them starved to death.
(Chops up more vegetables.)

GRACE

There were millions starving to death even before the plague.

ADAM

I doubt there's more than a handful now. Scattered.

GRACE

(Long pause.) I remember reading studies of mitochondrial DNA. Man was close to extinction 75000 years ago. There may've been only a few dozen women to reproduce. Living in Africa.

ADAM

So, all mankind's descended from a few women then?

GRACE

That's right. And studies show they spread all over the world from there. To Asia, all over Europe, across the land bridge to North America from Siberia, down to South America.

ADAM

And that took thousands of years, right? So, how come we had all this racist stuff when everyone was related by DNA? The people on Tristan are all shades and colors. They don't seem to have racism.

GRACE

(Long pause.) I guess it took a long time to develop this race thing. And I think the environment had something to do with it. In an exercise, when they asked people to stand next to each other on a big map based on DNA, there were all colors and shades together.

ADAM

That must have been a big surprise when they looked at each other.

GRACE

(She laughs.) I told you before race was just part of a bigger thing called discrimination. Some people need to look down on others. Someone to hate, someone to make themselves feel superior.

ADAM

Well, that might be solved now. Not too many people left to hate.

GRACE

(They work in silence.) Maybe we should help repopulate the world.

ADAM

It'd take more than us.

GRACE

We could do our part. I'm still young.

ADAM

We have enough trouble feeding ourselves.

GRACE

We could fix up our hay filled bedroom. Make it more romantic.

Silence. He chops up last of vegetables, replaces lid and stokes fire.

ADAM

Where're the spices, salt and pepper?

GRACE

Over there. In my "cupboard", that hole in the hay. It's my job.

ADAM

What?

GRACE

To help repopulate the world.

ADAM

I thought you're a writer. That's your job!

GRACE

(Laughs.) That's my other job.

He also laughs. She has gotten his humor back.

ADAM

Pretty good at your job. Both of 'em.

GRACE

I've got a few good years left. *(Coyly.)* We could have lots of kids, don't you think? *(Silence as he removes the lid and checks the stew, then stokes fire.)*

ADAM

You were teaching before the pandemic. Why'd you want to write?

GRACE

I always wanted to write but I needed something to do to live.

ADAM

What did you do?

GRACE

Got a job on an island up north. I was starving.

ADAM

Good reason.

GRACE

Taught all grades, all subjects in a tiny school. Lived in a little place.

ADAM

At least it was home!

GRACE

Some home! That didn't last long. I had to go inland.

ADAM

Why? Because of the pandemic?

GRACE

Yes. Everyone left that hadn't died. I was the last to leave.

ADAM

And then you headed south?

GRACE

Yep. That was the end of my dream of being a writer or a journalist.

ADAM

You still can be! But now we've got to get on with living.

GRACE

Surviving, you mean. Haven't written a thing in a long time.

ADAM

You're writin' now, aren't you?

GRACE

Yeh, sure! I don't even have paper to write on. A few old pencils.

ADAM

Reminds me of Rodin. He used scraps of paper and charcoal.

GRACE

When'll you get me some scrap paper?

ADAM

(*Impatiently*) You think it grows on trees? (*Calms down*) Look, next time I go to one of the dumps, I'll find you something to write on.

GRACE

Any kind of paper will do as long as it isn't rotten.

ADAM

I'll find some wrapped in plastic.

GRACE

Maybe there's some in a wrecked store I saw coming here.

ADAM

Strange, isn't it? The greatest legacy of civilization will be all those dumps, those mounds spread across the wasteland. (*Turns on radio.*)

GRACE

Nature will cover them up. Hidden for years. Like the Mayan ruins.

SFX. Radio crackling and whistling looking for a transmission.

ADAM

Don't understand it. Must be someone out there. Somewhere.

GRACE

Maybe there is and you're not picking it up.

ADAM

If there was, I'd hear a different sound.

SFX. More sounds of radio noises. He turns it off.

GRACE

(Sigh) It's been such a long time since I had a safe secure home.

ADAM

I know but don't blame me for that!

GRACE

I'm not!

ADAM

When I found you in the blizzard along the trail in a ditch, you were ragged and homeless, and nearly dead. I've done my best.

GRACE

I know. I was exhausted! I was frozen. I was hungry! *(Sobs.)*

ADAM

If you had a white face, I wouldn't have seen you. You'd be dead.

Her sobs turn to laughs.

GRACE

If we didn't have a blizzard and I fell, then I'd still be in that ditch?

ADAM

I would have seen you and picked you up.

GRACE

That's reassuring! *(He puts his arms around her and hugs her.)*

ADAM

This is home! Longest I've been in any one place in years.

GRACE

When are we going to find a place that we can stay in?

ADAM

We will, we will. Be patient!

GRACE

I want to settle down, have a nice home, raise a family.

SFX: He throws the poker against the grate with a clang.

ADAM

Stop complaining. We're lucky to be alive! I've been on the move since this pandemic started. You think I like this any more than you?

ADAM

(He stirs stew.) Wish we had some meat for this stew. Where is she?

GRACE

She went to get carrots.

ADAM

I'm worried they'll catch her. No telling what they'd do to her.

GRACE

Don't worry. No one's caught her in all those years on the run.

ADAM

There's always a first time.

GRACE

She's clever, cunning like a fox. She can take care of herself.

ADAM

Smells trouble miles away, like a wild animal. Still, I worry.

GRACE

Don't worry. She's learned what she needs to know – to survive.

ADAM

She was so young when it started. Never had a chance.

GRACE

What do you mean?

ADAM

I mean like us, to be educated, learn about history, art and science.

GRACE

Why does she need to know that? It's no use anymore.

ADAM

You could teach her some of that. Besides, it might be useful one day. If we ever had children, wouldn't you want them to be educated? To study art, music, science, history, and other things?

GRACE

Yes, but how? With what? It would be wonderful to have a school again, but we'd need books and all sorts of things. *(Sarcastically.)* Of course, we'll use all the paper and pens and pencils you got me.

ADAM

(Ignores her.) We still have museums some places. There must still be paintings and sculptures not destroyed that we could go find one day when it becomes safe. And there must still be books in libraries that haven't been burned down or destroyed.

GRACE

You are a dreamer. Just a little while ago, you were talking about working from dawn to dusk, trying to survive, and now you're running a school for the children we don't have yet.

ADAM

I know surviving comes first but we all have to dream. I could teach science things and you could teach art and history. Couldn't you teach her some of that now?

GRACE

Wish I had one of those computers we used to have.

ADAM

What good'll that do? No electricity anymore. I'll get you that paper.

He paces back and forth as if a caged animal.

GRACE

Why are you so jumpy? You're nervous as a cat.

ADAM

Thought I heard something out there again.

GRACE

It's just her coming back. Or maybe the cougar again.

SFX: A distant sound of a single rifle shot to the west, down river.

ADAM

That was a shot! Far away! I'm going up! *(He rushes across floor.)*

GRACE

Be careful. Don't need you shot up.

He leaves. She stops writing, listens. He slides back down.

ADAM

Nothing! I was sure I heard it! Down river! *(Checks fire and stew.)*

GRACE

I'm glad it was nothing! *(Softens.)* Why are you so worried?

ADAM

They've been looking for me.

GRACE

What're you talking about?

ADAM

They heard about me, how I grow food. They don't know how to.

GRACE

You don't know that. They brought the pandemic.

ADAM

We don't know that.

GRACE

(Hatred.) Well, I do.

ADAM

The pandemic was already here. They looked for an isolated place.

GRACE

Maybe it was a different virus but they brought it in by ship.

ADAM

We don't know that either.

GRACE

They killed our people with those high-powered rifles. They took our land. Those invaders destroyed my life!

ADAM

The pandemic spread and killed people. The land was empty. They survived somehow and just wanted to farm. What's wrong with that?

GRACE

(Calms down.) All they know is how to harvest hay and that's not farming. What a joke! Farmers! One old cow. Horses. *(Long pause)*

ADAM

If she's not back soon, I'm going out. *(Paces.)* I'm really worried.

GRACE

Don't be. She's the other way. Up river!

ADAM

She might have gone back down river. Maybe they saw her.

GRACE

We're too close to the farmers. Let's get far away.

ADAM

I agree. We'll have to move soon, but that's not so easy to do.

Turns radio on. **SFX.** *Radio crackling sounds.*

GRACE
Why do you keep fiddling with that? No one's there.

ADAM
There has to be someone out there.

SFX. *There are more radio sounds. He turns it off.*

GRACE
Think she'll stay with us?

ADAM
I'll ask her. Maybe.

GRACE
She's ready to settle down with her own nest.

ADAM
I agree. Pretty soon.

GRACE
But she needs another bird before she builds that nest.

ADAM
There aren't many other birds around.

GRACE
(Noise from above.) Someone's coming.

Grace cocks the shotgun. Adam douses lights.

End of Scene One.

Scene Two. *Grace and Adam next to tunnel entrance. Sly enters.*

GRACE

There you are.

SLY

Did you see the cougar? He was beautiful.

ADAM

We heard him, or her. Chased it away.

SLY

Got the carrots. Brought radishes as well. Want anything else?

ADAM

Well, if you find any wine out there…!

GRACE

Listen to the man, will you? A real connoisseur! For the stew of course! It's been so long since anyone made wine.

ADAM

I could make wine. If I could find an old vineyard, maybe I could get the grapevines back in shape.

GRACE

I remember some vineyards on some of the islands where we're going. Those were the days! Wine and cheese and bread!

ADAM

All gone! When we find a safe refuge, I could grow wheat. I'd have to learn a bit about making cheese

GRACE

I'll help you make bread. Let me think about cheese.

SLY

Oh, I'd love some bread. Milk and bread. I'd be so happy with that.

GRACE

I'll look for some grain. Maybe there's some left.

ADAM

All I've seen is hay. *(Grace moves away.)* You goin' somewhere?

GRACE

Need a nature break. Bet that old silo up river has some grain. Be right back.

ADAM

Be careful. You never know what's out there.

GRACE

Don't worry. I'm pretty clever too.

ADAM

And bring some cheese back with you.

GRACE

Sure, why not! To go with the bread and wine? *(She exits.)*

SLY

Don't remember ever drinking wine. My special treat's milk, when I can find it. I've been on the run so much I hardly get much of that.

ADAM

If I had wine, I'd toast your anniversary, but here's something better!

He crosses hay covered floor and gets some milk from behind a bale.

ADAM

Fresh this morning, chilled in the stream!

SLY

Oh, you're wonderful! You remembered about the milk!

ADAM

I made three cups for us. We'll have a toast together.

She gives him a brief hug. He moves away from her embrace.

ADAM

Take it easy. Hard to believe you've been with us only one month.

SLY

It seems like more. This is the longest I've stayed anywhere.

ADAM

You think you want to go with us? Stay with us? We'll move soon.

SLY

I'd like to. Where will we go?

ADAM

Good question. Wish I knew. Away from danger.

She sits on log. Long silence. He is lost in thought.

SLY

What's wrong?

ADAM

It's a wasteland out there! As if millions of swarms of tiny locusts...

She moves close to him. She speaks gently.

SLY

Don't, Adam. It'll be alright.

His voice wavers. As he talks, she is close, lightly caressing him.

ADAM

(His voice wavers.) Corruption, lawlessness, then so many died, from the pandemics, starvation, *(pause)* then war... *(He drifts off.)*

SLY

That turned things upside down.

ADAM

After you were born, even before, we treated others like animals.

SLY

So, we lost our right to feel superior?

ADAM

Our moral imperative. Corruption, even then, from the highest level.

SLY

That's what I meant.

ADAM

And now we're the animals! They're the hunters. *(Long pause.)*

SLY

I feel like a wild animal. You've seen those wild cats? I feel like one.

ADAM

Feral cats! They're savage! They live in a burrow, in the ground.

SLY

That's what I want. My own hole in the ground, my nest.

ADAM

I hear a noise. Must be Grace.

SFX. *Sound above. She moves away. Grace slides down to floor.*

GRACE

No grain! Just rats. *(Pause.)* And I didn't see any people out there!

SLY

What about a cat? We could use one. A female. And a male cat too.
Cats always need another cat to play with and keep them company.
We'd soon have many mouths to feed.

GRACE

Nope. But I agree. I sometimes think I hear mice scurrying around.
But what about that cougar? Nice kitty! Here, kitty, kitty.

SLY

Funny.

ADAM

That can wait. We've been waiting for you, Grace. Take this cup.

He pours milk into three cups.

GRACE

What's this for?

ADAM

Sly. A celebration. One month with us. Let's toast! To your health.

They raise cups and toast her.

ADAM

(To Grace.) And soon, it'll be three months in this burrow.

GRACE

And even longer in that first barn after you found me in a ditch.

ADAM

You were on your way to see your sister. Sorry about that.

SLY

You didn't find her?

GRACE

I found her. She died. Then I came back to the barn.

ADAM

(Quietly.) Well, anyway, you've been with me many months.

GRACE

Seems as if we've been together forever.

They raise their cups again and toast to that.

SLY

I'm very happy here. I feel as if I have a family, a home.

GRACE

We feel the same way. We hope you stay with us.

ADAM

This stew could use something. Any more parsnips or turnips left?

SLY

Just a few. I'll get 'em. Everything else's gone except potatoes.

ADAM

Anything'll help this pot. Be careful out there! It's dark.

SLY

Don't worry. I'm a night animal. I can see in the dark. (*Dashes out.*)

Grace gets up, lifts lid on pot. Puts it back.

GRACE

The stew's nice but we need protein. Wish we had meat or fish for it.

ADAM

I could look for fish in the river.

GRACE

That river's been polluted for years. Try the fresh water streams.

ADAM

Should be a few fish there. Next time I'll get one for dinner!

SFX. Rifle shot to west, followed by another. Silence. They freeze.

GRACE

(*Quietly.*) He didn't leave. You were right about that other one.

ADAM

They must've seen 'er.

GRACE

She's on the other side of the barn. She's too smart to be seen.

ADAM

She's in trouble. I've got to go out. *(He runs to tunnel exit.)*

GRACE

Wait! Someone's coming! *(They freeze. They kill any lights.)*

SFX. People approaching above. Voices speak in foreign accents.

VOICE 1

He headed this way but I lost track of 'im.

VOICE 2

It's getting pretty dark. It'll be hard to find him.

SFX. Sound of voices receding. Sound of running, then shouting.

VOICE 1

There he goes!

SFX. Sound of rifle shot to south west side of barn.

VOICE 2

I think I got him. Where'd he go?

VOICE 1

Down near the river. Into the reeds.

VOICE 2

We'll never find him in the dark. He can't go far! Let's come back.

VOICE 1

Hold on a minute! He was heading for the barn. Shine your light.

SFX. Sound of them in the barn entrance above.

VOICE 2

There's nothing but hay here. Let's check the other sides.

SFX. Sounds encircling barn to north, then back (east) then around. As they turn to the back of the barn, sound of the cougar snarling.

VOICE 1
Watch out. It's a cougar.

SFX. Sound of horses neighing. Cougar snarling. Horses galloping.
SFX. Sound of them leaving to west. Sounds diminish.

ADAM
A close call! Glad that cougar was still hanging around.

GRACE
They were talking about a man, not a woman.

ADAM
Maybe they thought she was a man. Sounds as if they got her.

GRACE
I was wrong. Go find her! (*She pushes him.*) Wait! I hear someone.

Grace grabs shotgun. Adam grabs knife. Che slides down heavily.

ADAM
Who're you? Don't move!

Sly slides down tunnel and lands lightly on floor.

SLY
Put that gun away and knife away. They were after him. The cougar ran away.

GRACE
That's what the shooting was all about? After him?

SLY
When I saw him heading this way, I ducked into the reeds.

ADAM
Think they saw you?

SLY
Don't think so, but I didn't want to give away the barn.

ADAM

What's your name?

CHE

My name is Che. *(He moans in slight pain.)*

GRACE

What's wrong with him?

SLY

They shot him. He's hit in the leg.

ADAM

How bad is it?

CHE

I don't know. I can still walk but it hurts like hell. A flesh wound.

ADAM

Let's see it. Sit on that bale. Roll up your pants leg. What happened?

Che sits on a bale of hay, rolls up his pants leg and continues.

CHE

They saw me a mile from here. I outran their horses but I forgot about those powerful guns.

GRACE

You took off, you say? Headed this way?

CHE

When I saw her, thought I'd be safer in the reeds. They saw me.

ADAM

They'll be back early. We only have a few hours.

GRACE

Let me do that, Adam.

Adam gets out of the way. Grace stoops down.

SLY
Is there anything I can do to help?

She gets very close to Che and hovers over him.

GRACE
Sure, Sly. Help me fix him up. Get that rag over there. And that kit.

Sly gets a rag and the kit from behind bale.

GRACE
Sorry we don't have much first aid stuff. Just this old camping kit.

Sly opens First Aid kit, rummages around, gets bandage and gauze.

SLY
There's a bandage left. I'll use it.

ADAM
This's what's left of our National Health Care System!

SLY
Grace, I'll take care of him. You have to look after the stew.

Sly pushes Grace gently toward the stew pot.

SLY
I'll take care of you. Sit still. You hurt anywhere? *(She touches him and checks him out.)*

CHE
I'm alright.

ADAM
Where'd you come from?

CHE
From the coast.

ADAM

You see anyone on the way here?

CHE

No. It was strange. I think everyone's dead. Saw lots of graves.

GRACE

No people? No bodies?

CHE

Nope. Saw lots of cougars. Wild dogs. Vultures. Everything's empty, rundown, overgrown.

SLY

You can get up and test your leg.

He gets up and walks slowly around as talk continues.

ADAM

Where're you headed?

CHE

Before I left the coast, two old folks told me about a group camped up in the mountains. They were telling me how to get there, but died together before my eyes. I couldn't help. Just stayed a distance away.

ADAM

Sad. It gets old people faster. What do you know about this group?

CHE

An abandoned village. Old houses. Lots of barns. A large group. Hope they're still alive.

SLY

And if not? We might be the only ones still left?

GRACE

Except for the farmers. Don't forget them.

ADAM

I'll try that radio again. Must be someone out there.

GRACE

Hurry. We need to get moving and get outta here.

SFX. Sound of him turning dial, crackling and whistling of radio.

CHE

Nothing? I'm not surprised. *(SFX. Radio clicking off.)*

ADAM

Tell me more about this group. They might've survived the plague.

CHE

Good spring water, not polluted. They feel safe there. Food's a big problem. They fish, but don't know a thing about growing food. They gather nuts, berries, fruit, anything to eat.

GRACE

Just like the native peoples did, before the European invasion.

ADAM

(Intense.) What about grains, wheat, corn? They know about those?

CHE

Not that I know of. Must be fighting starvation.

ADAM

(To Grace, excitedly.) I could help them. Teach them farming!

CHE

You do that! But I'm going to start a small guerrilla group there.

GRACE

What kind of talk is all this? We don't even know if anyone's alive.

CHE

It's our best bet. Our only bet. We've got to leave.

SLY

Still want the parsnips and turnips? Might even be a rutabaga or two.

GRACE

Alright, hurry! No telling when we'll eat again. How far do we go?

CHE

Two weeks hiking. Follow the river upstream. *(Sly starts to leave.)*

CHE

(To Sly) Wait. I'll go with you. *(They exit.)*

GRACE

Maybe she's found that bird for her nest.

ADAM

That's good, but the sooner we leave the better. Let's start packing.

GRACE

You're right. Shouldn't take chances. I'll save this stew for later.

ADAM

Stew tastes better with age anyway.

GRACE

I couldn't enjoy it now. I'd rather eat on the road, when it's safer.

ADAM

Better check the radio one last time. *(He turns it on.)*

SFX. Radio crackling then he stops. B/G light static from radio.

They pack up, drain pot, put vegetables in a bag and stow the pot.

GRACE

I'm putting the bag of vegetables in my pack and the pot with yours.

ADAM

I'll find water later. We have a few hours, but they won't follow.

GRACE
Not even when they discover this burrow of ours?

ADAM
We'll have too much of a start. They won't know which way to go.

GRACE
I hope this new place is really safe. I want a home, to settle down and raise children, lots of them. And educate them.

ADAM
And have a real farm, a vegetable garden, a wheat field! Lots of animals, of all kinds and shapes and sizes.

GRACE
A real community! Of all shapes and sizes, *(slight pause)* and shades of color. Finally, something to hope for! We'll call it Cascadia!

Sly and Che rush back and slide down the hay tunnel.

CHE
You're wrong. They didn't wait 'til morning. They're headed here!

ADAM
You sure? They're away from the river? *(Urgently)* You're positive?

CHE
Yes. We saw a light to the west, down river. They're heading toward our entrance above.

Adam moves hay bale from spot in floor.

ADAM
I thought this might come in handy someday. My escape hatch!

He pries up a couple of boards from floor.

CHE
Where does it go?

ADAM

Away from them! Take everything you can and head into the reeds.

CHE

Won't they see us out there?

ADAM

Keep in the shadow of the barn so their light doesn't reach you.

SLY

What'll we do in the reeds? They'll find us there!

ADAM

I'll be right behind you. I have a small boat hidden nearby.

CHE

What then? Are we going to row it up river? Dangerous.

ADAM

We'll get across the river while they're busy here. Let's go!

They all grab packs and loose things and run to exit on hay floor.

GRACE

Follow me, Sly.

Grace steps down through escape hatch onto steps.

ADAM

I'll pass your pack down, Sly. Quickly. Grab the radio, will you Che?

Sly steps down through escape hatch onto steps.

CHE

Alright. Give me that shotgun. You go ahead. I'll be right behind.

ADAM

What're you going to do?

CHE

Delay them a bit. Go. Hurry.

ADAM

And torch the barn. That'll keep them busy. *(He leaves.)*

CHE

(He mumbles.) I can play the game too.

Che cocks the shotgun and shuffles to tunnel.

SFX. Approaching footsteps heard along with voices of two men, gradually becoming audible, speaking with "foreign" accents.

VOICE 1

See that loose bale of hay! Help me move it.

SFX. Bale of hay being moved above, and flung onto nearby floor.

VOICE 1

It's a tunnel! Let's go down! Shoot if you see anything move!

VOICE 2

I don't know. It's so narrow. Wait! I thought I heard a noise.

VOICE 1

It's nothing. Get in there. I'll be right behind. Watch out! He's got a gun!

SFX. Shotgun fired. Someone yelling in pain, falling. Delay. Rifle fired followed by shotgun. Someone falling. Someone sliding down tunnel. Che holds shotgun and two rifles, which he admires.

CHE

That should delay those bastards. Permanently! And these rifles could come in handy.

He moans in pain. Sly comes up through escape hatch.

SLY

Che! I heard shots. What happened?

CHE

I had some business to take care of. *(Involuntary moan.)*

SLY

You're hurt. You've been shot.

CHE

I'll be alright. Go get Adam. Tell him it's alright to come back.

SLY

Don't move. I'll be right back to care for you. *(She exits down.)*

SFX. Radio crackling. Sounds become clear. Morse code is heard. (Dash dot dash dot, dash dash dot dash.) CQ – Calling anyone, over and over, followed by Station ID.

SFX. CQ CQ CQ DE ABC ABC AR.

CHE

(Yells.) Adam, come quickly. It's the radio, the call signal. There's someone out there!

End of Scene Two.

End of Act One.

ACT TWO

Scene One: A month later. Lighting dims slowly as night arrives.

SFX: Winter. Wind whistling around corners, thru slats and rattling of boards. Radio being tested. Nothing comes in. Stew pot over fire.

ADAM
Nothing. Don't get it. If Che heard a CQ why don't they keep at it?

GRACE
Maybe their batteries are low. What's a CQ?

ADAM
Calling anyone. They want whoever hears to respond. I'll try later.

GRACE
Where're Sly and Che? It's over a month. Maybe they stayed.

ADAM
Che said he'd come back no matter what.

GRACE
It's getting cold.

ADAM
Feels like snow.

SFX: Sound of radio as Adam tries to receive something. Nothing.

GRACE
You said you'd wait until later. Build up the fire. It's freezing.

ADAM
I suppose it's dark enough.

He removes the grate and puts logs in fire then puts grate back.

GRACE
What'll you do if someone comes on? Those batteries are dead.

ADAM

We found a generator downstream, and gas. In an abandoned store. Good for a few hours.

GRACE

Why not use solar panels? To charge batteries. Lots of them around.

ADAM

Someone will spot them. But I put a small aerial on the metal roof. Good for five hundred miles.

GRACE

Do it now. When it's night. You know the frequency they're on.

ADAM

When I hear something. No telling who might receive a CQ.

GRACE

Suit yourself. When you searched downstream, you found no one.

ADAM

I hear something.

SFX: Faint sound of hoof beats coming closer, louder and louder.

GRACE

Horses.

ADAM

Must be them. 'Bout time. Let's be careful. Douse the lights.

GRACE

(She does.) Wonder why it took them so long.

ADAM

Must've been some trouble. Don't move.

SFX: Sound of horses neighing, then Che and Sly slide down floor.

GRACE

Glad to see you. We've been worried.

ADAM

She was. I wasn't. How's the community? You find it?

CHE

Yep. All dead. Graves everywhere. Some bones. Overgrown.

SLY

You're right about the food. It looks as if most of them died from various forms of the pandemic diseases, and then the rest starved to death. We brought you back a note.

CHE

Written by the last survivor. Read it.

ADAM

(Reads.) Tell our story. Everyone dead. I'll be gone soon. Tried to raise food but failed. Lost our crops. Severe winter then drought. People starving to death. New people brought deadly flus that spread fast. First the old folks, then the children died. Couldn't do a thing. Cattle also died, went mad. The water polluted. Doc went early, said we had many diseases, all kinds, that spread before symptoms seen, we couldn't control. No food. God save our souls. Amen. Deacon.

SLY

Horrible. If they didn't die from the plague, they starved to death.

ADAM

He said many diseases. That's what I thought. What kept you?

CHE

Ran into heavy snow 'bout half way back. Holed up in an old house.

SLY

There was even an old bed still there.

GRACE

I see why you were delayed.

SLY

If everyone's gone, isn't it our job to repopulate the planet?

GRACE

With only two of us it'll take a long time. Adam, what do you think?

ADAM

(Ignores her.) You didn't see anyone up and back?

CHE

Not a soul. Just more graves and bones along the way. Dead animals too. Cows and horses and sheep. I think they starved to death.

ADAM

Nothing living?

CHE

Cougars now and then, and coyotes and foxes. A lot of wild animals.

GRACE

Stands to reason. Without people, wild animals should increase.

SLY

Not all of them. Not many raccoons. Saw some wild dog packs.

Sly has been showing increasing signs of exhaustion and sickness.

CHE

And a grizzly. Sly, you need to get some sleep. You're not too well.

ADAM

What's wrong with her?

GRACE

(Grace touches her forehead.) No fever.

SLY

I'm alright. Let's move to the old house over there. No one around.

GRACE

Adam's afraid someone might still come. Looking for those guys.

CHE

After all this? Adam, we didn't see a soul. We rode miles.

ADAM

We'll move there soon. Not yet. Where're the horses?

CHE

Tied up. Where should I put them?

ADAM

I found a shed close by. Come, I'll show you. They'll keep the old cow company.

SLY

Any milk? I'm famished. I need to drink something.

GRACE

Drink some of this fresh spring water. Adam, do we have any milk?

ADAM

A bit. I'll get more. But the cow's not long for the world though.

SLY

We passed a goat and kid before we got here. And a couple of lambs.

CHE

We'll go get 'em in the morning.

ADAM

That'd be great. Maybe we can have that lamb stew after all.

SLY

Cute little lambs. How could you?

CHE

Baaa! Baaa!

ADAM

Let's go. Look after the fire, will you? *(They exit. Grace stokes fire.)*

SLY

It's really cold. Snow'll reach here soon. Che was right. I'm sick.

GRACE

You're just cold. I'll build up the fire a bit more. It's pitch black outside. No one'll see the smoke. *(She stokes fire.)*

SLY

Grace, I brought back another lost stray. She's back there in the hay.

GRACE

What do you mean? Who?

SLY

I call her Pandi. She's also starved. *(A plaintive "mew" off.)*

GRACE

A cat? Guess we can handle one more mouth.

SLY

She's a kitten, a Bengal. She needs some milk before we lose her.

GRACE

I'll take care of that. *(She exits to feed Pandi.)*

SLY

Why is Adam still so worried? *(Grace returns.)*

GRACE

He can't believe we're alone. Expects someone any moment.

SLY

Che thinks we should just go find them and wipe them out.

GRACE

They'll work that out. They're stubborn. Really strong opinions.

SLY

How're we fixed for food? I'm starved. We ran out some days ago.

GRACE

Thought you could live on love.

SLY

That just makes me hungrier.

GRACE

We'll have milk from that cow. And lots of potatoes.

SLY

And meat?

GRACE

Not 'til you and Che bring back those lambs. Those cute lambs. Baa!

SLY

I suppose if I don't think about it, and if I'm starved enough.

GRACE

And now we have another mouth to feed.

SLY

You mean Pandi? She has a small mouth. And besides, I expect she will make up for it. I've heard mice scratching around in the hay.

GRACE

Better add to that stew. Look behind that hay bale, will you?
(She adds a few vegetables, while Sly slowly moves a bale.)

SLY

Wow! Lots of food here. It's like a cupboard, and full of vegetables.

GRACE

I made a little room and Adam searched for any food he could find.

SLY

Enough for a couple of months?

GRACE

At least until the new root crops come up.

SLY

He plans to stay awhile?

GRACE

He wasn't sure what you two would find up there.

SLY

He must've guessed. Glad he did the planting.

SFX. Wind whistling around corners of barn, increasing in strength.

GRACE

Wind's starting to whip up. Gonna be a cold night.

SLY

Wonder if it's snowing yet.

GRACE

Take a look. Move that bale aside.

Sly moves bale to floor with a plunk and looks out. Wind stronger.

SLY

Wow! The snow's blowing through the slats.

GRACE

What's it look like out there?

SLY

Too dark to see. Must be wild. Not fit for man nor beast.

She tries to lift the bale back in place but can't. Grace comes over and helps her lift it back up.

GRACE

You really are sick. You need food and plenty of rest.

SLY

I'll be alright if I just get something to eat.

GRACE

Hope the guys get back soon.

SLY

Could they get lost in the dark?

GRACE

It's not very far away. But I'll feel better when they come back.

SFX. Sound of someone returning. Feet on floor above.

SLY

You got your wish. They're back.

GRACE

Someday the wrong one might come down. We're taking a chance.

SLY

We need a signal. I'll work on it with Che.

GRACE

Good idea.

Che slides down and lands with a plunk.

SLY

No need to worry. Here he is.

GRACE

Where's Adam?

CHE

Milking the cow. She perked up when the horses joined 'er.

GRACE

Do you think she'll last the winter?

CHE

Doubt it.

GRACE

Good thing you're getting that goat. We'll need some milk.

SFX. Wind whistling around corners of barn. It increases.

CHE

I hope they survive. We saw the lambs near a shed next to the trail.

GRACE

I hope they stay put and don't wander.

SFX. Footsteps growing louder. Crunch of snow. Stamping feet.

SLY

It's Adam.

He slides down slowly and drops a pail on floor with a clank.

ADAM

Here's your milk. Didn't spill a drop.

SLY

Thank heavens. I've dreamed of milk. Haven't had any for days.

He pours milk into a cup and gives it to her. She gulps it down.

ADAM

Easy, now, easy.

SLY

I guess I'm a bit primitive. I'll be more civilized with the stew.
(Sly poured some milk into a dish, and put it near two hay bales.)

SLY

Pandi. Pandi. *(She speaks softly.)* Have you been catching mice?

Pandi peeks out slowly from between the bales, looks warily around, sees Sly, then begins to lap the milk. Sly pats her and she purrs. She slurps the milk quickly and disappears.

SFX. *Strong wind gusts buffeting the barn. Whistling loudly.*

ADAM
How's dinner coming? *(He peers into the stew as Grace stirs it.)*

GRACE
Be done soon.

ADAM
Sly'll need to fill up. She's on empty.

SLY
What's it like out there? Snow was coming through the slats.

ADAM
A full-blown blizzard's coming in.

SFX. *More sounds of wind increasing in strength.*

CHE
Wind's already forming snowdrifts.

SLY
We can't go get the lambs and goats now.

ADAM
Don't worry. They won't go anywhere.

GRACE
Stew's about ready. Get a bowl from my cupboard.

Sly shuffles across floor and picks up four wooden bowls.

SLY
Where'd you get those?

GRACE

Made 'em while you were gone.

She fills the bowls with stew.

SLY

You're turning into a regular pioneer woman.

GRACE

We're all becoming pioneers, like it or not.

CHE

Adam and I've been talking. About going downstream.

GRACE

You went there already.

SLY

You went ten miles last time. Isn't that far enough?

CHE

No, we mean much further. Fifty, a hundred miles.

GRACE

This weather is terrible. It's dangerous. I don't like the idea.

SLY

That's half way to the sea.

CHE

We know.

GRACE

Why do you need to go? You might run into more guys with guns.

ADAM

We're gonna need some livestock. Another cow, coupla horses.

CHE

Wish we could find a good Border Collie to help herd.

ADAM

And how about chickens? Laying hens?

SLY

That'd be nice. What about a rooster? Won't we need one of those?

CHE

Anything we can bring back, maybe even another lamb.

SLY

I hope so. If those two lambs are boy/girl you're not touching the wool on their backs.

CHE

Not even wool? Nice warm wool on a cold winter day?

SLY

Well, as long as it doesn't interfere with repopulating our animals.

Sly slowly goes off to side room, touches her forehead, stumbles.

CHE

A nice wool blanket would be nice. *(He follows her off.)* For you.

ADAM

I'm worried about Sly. Do you think she's got one of the viruses?

GRACE

If she did, they'd both have died on the way back. Forget about it.

ADAM

Not necessarily. That note said it takes a while to get symptoms. Before that, you can infect others. The virus spreads quickly.

GRACE

So, we could all be infected with a form of pandemic virus?

ADAM

Possibly. I guess you're right. No one else seems sick. I'll forget it.

GRACE

I don't think she has a pandemic virus.

ADAM

She's definitely sick. Maybe just the flu. It's winter, after all.

GRACE

When do you think you'll leave?

SFX. Wind whistling with slight decrease in strength.

ADAM

Soon as there's a letup in the blizzard.

Che returns. Eats more stew.

CHE

She just needs rest. This stew's good. Really tasty.

GRACE

Parsnips, leeks, rutabagas. That's the flavor.

CHE

These look like beans here. What are they?

GRACE

Lentils. Found some dried ones. In a house with a pantry.

CHE

Delicious!

GRACE

(Long pause) Che, how long'll you be gone?

CHE

Couple of days, if the weather's not too bad.

ADAM

Will you two fetch the lambs and goats while we're gone?

GRACE

Sure thing.

ADAM

Che, Sly looks terrible. Think she picked up something on the trip?

CHE

Like the plague? Forget it. She's just exhausted. She'll be alright.

GRACE

She's just cold and hungry. We should take her some stew. She'll recover with a good night's sleep.

Grace fills a bowl and disappears to give it to Sly.

SFX. *Wind decreasing. Becoming a slight breeze. Static on radio.*

ADAM

Think I'll try the radio again. Wind's let up. *(He tries frequencies.)*

CHE

I'll build up the fire. Gonna be a cold night.

SFX. *Static on radio stops and the pattern of CQs come in slowly.*

SFX. *CQ CQ CQ DE ABC ABC AR.*

CHE

That's it! That's what I heard before.

ADAM

That's a CQ all right. Calling anyone.

GRACE

(Grace returns.) What're you gonna do?

ADAM

Guess we'll take a chance. Help me with the generator.

                              CHE
Where is it?

                              ADAM
Behind that bale.

Che shuffles and drags the generator across the floor.

                              CHE
Got it! And the gas.

                              ADAM
Fill it up and start it.

Che pours gas into generator and tries several times before it starts.

                              CHE
There she goes. Transmitter hooked up.

SFX. *Generator idling quietly. Another CQ coming in very weakly.*

SFX. *CQ (Pause) CQ (Pause) CQ.*

                              ADAM
That's strange. He's altered the pattern. It's slower.

                              CHE
He's faltering. It's irregular.

SFX. *Another CQ but even slower and weaker. CQ.*

                              GRACE
He's running out of power.

                              CHE
Or getting weak from starvation.

                              GRACE
Why doesn't he use his voice instead of these signals? It's faster.

ADAM

First of all, it takes much more energy to transmit voice than to use simple Morse code. They might not have that much energy from the generator. Or themselves. But I don't think that's the only reason.

GRACE

What do you mean?

ADAM

They want to remain anonymous. With voice you provide too much information.

CHE

Maybe it's a she. Doesn't want to reveal that.

GRACE

Or maybe you don't speak English. Or you're lying. Here's another.

SFX. *(Morse from ABC) CQ (Long Pause) DE ABC (Pause) AR.*

CHE

Respond, Adam. Before they sign off.

ADAM

Here goes. Gotta take a chance.

SFX. *BBC: ABC DE BBC BBC KN.*

SFX. *ABC: QTH MTH WD RIV = OP IS SAM KN.*

CHE

It's faster. It's as if he'd given up hope. Now he sounds excited.

SFX. *BBC: QTH UP RIV = NAME IS ADAM = HW WD K.*

SFX. *ABC: SEV KM K.*

GRACE

What'd he say?

ADAM

His name is Sam. He's located at the mouth of a wide river. I'm pretty sure it's our big river.

SFX. BBC: WHT SIDE K.

SFX. ABC: N K.

SFX. BBC: RU OK K

SFX. ABC: N FUD = WEAK K.

CHE

And now? What'd he say?

ADAM

Our side of the river. You were right, Che. He's starving and weak.

SFX. BBC: HW MNY K.

SFX. ABC: 2 K.

ADAM

There're two of them.

GRACE

Must be a trap. Probably a whole group.

CHE

I don't think so. Ask about the weather there.

SFX. BBC: WX K.

SFX. ABC: LT SN K.

SFX. BBC: TK TRL NSIDE K.

SFX. ABC: K.

SFX. BBC: SK.

SFX. ABC: SN CL.

GRACE
What'd he say?

ADAM
Snowing. We can't wait for a letup. They won't survive a blizzard.

CHE
If we're going to go, now's the time.

SFX. Periodic sounds of wind still whistling and snow blowing.

GRACE
What if I'm right? What if it's a trap?

ADAM
I've thought of that. Che, get one of those rifles.

CHE
I've only found a dozen shells.

ADAM
Bring 'em all. Wait. On second thought, leave a few.

CHE
Why?

ADAM
Grace and Sly might need a few.

CHE
The other rifle?

ADAM
Grace, we're gonna leave one rifle and the pistol.

CHE
Only six shots in the pistol.

ADAM

That'll be enough.

GRACE

What're we gonna need guns for?

ADAM

I hope a mountain lion didn't get Sly's little lambies.

GRACE

He might be hungry but not as hungry as her.

ADAM

That's the attitude. This is survival.

GRACE

How long before you'll be back?

ADAM

Couple of days. Depends on how weak they are.

CHE

We're gonna carry them back?

ADAM

How else? Got a better idea?

GRACE

Drag 'em in the snow?

ADAM

Funny. We're leaving before dawn. If Sly's better, you two better do the same. Leave early to get those lambs and goats.

CHE

And look out for us. We'll be hungry when we get back.

GRACE

Two more mouths to feed.

ADAM

One last thing, Che. Fill up those wineskins with milk.

CHE

All four?

ADAM

Yep. And eat another bowl of stew before we leave.

CHE

Sure thing!

ADAM

And get some sleep. No telling when you'll have either.

CHE

I'll see how Sly's doing.

SLY

(Off) I'm fine. Come on in. *(Che exits.)*

ADAM

Grace, you can handle it?

GRACE

Are you kidding? Remember, I'm a pioneer woman.

End of Scene One.

Scene Two: *Two days later. Daylight but late in day. Gradually dims as it gets dark. Grace is chopping stew vegetables and stoking the fire with iron poker.*

SFX. *Wind whistles. Snow blowing. Distant stamp of boots. Knock — dah-di-dah.*

GRACE

That you Sly?

Grace cocks the pistol. Sly slides slowly down and drops the pail on the floor with a clank.

SLY

I did it! See, that wasn't so hard.

GRACE

What wasn't so hard? Not spilling a drop?

SLY

That, too. No, milking the cow. I'm getting to be a regular pioneer woman, too.

GRACE

You were almost a dead pioneer woman. You scared me. What was that knocking?

SLY

Didn't you know? That's our signal. Morse code. K for OK like the end of the messages.

GRACE

I see. You seemed to recover pretty quickly. I'm glad.

SLY

You all thought I had one of the pandemic viruses, didn't you?

GRACE

It did cross my mind, but if you did, I doubt you and Che would've made it back.

SLY

What would you have done if I had the plague? Throw me out?

GRACE

Of course not. We would've helped you recover.

SLY

Well, you needn't have worried. I'm pretty sure you only get it from people. Like, the living and dying.

GRACE

What do you think you had then?

SLY

Maybe a mild version of normal flu lingering around. Or I was just exhausted. Doesn't matter now. I'll be fine.

SFX. Sounds of howling wind as storm picks up intensity.

GRACE

I'm worried. The wind and snow are really picking up out there. Where are they?

SLY

Don't worry. They'll be back soon. They know what they're doing.

GRACE

It's two days. It's getting dark. I'll feel better when I hear those horses.

SLY

The stew hot? Just in case. You know what Che said.

GRACE

It is. I added another parsnip and leek. Steaming, and delicious.

SLY

We were lucky we got those critters before the storm got worse.

SLY

Now we know the sex of the two lambs. She's pregnant already.

GRACE

They got a start on us. They start young.

SLY

Wish we'd found a billygoat back there.

GRACE

Did you check out the sex of the kid? When he grows up?

SLY

That's incest!

GRACE

Not in their minds. Besides, how do you expect to repopulate?

SLY

How long before we have baby lambs?

GRACE

I don't know. Adam would know. Probably a few weeks.

SLY

When I was milking the cow, she looked so forlorn.

GRACE

A bull would perk her up, get her juices flowing again.

SLY

We're getting to be a Noah's Ark here, aren't we?

GRACE

I know a remote island up north. There's a deep bay where the English defended the place against the Americans. Rich farm land nearby, barns, and a mountaintop lookout for our army.

SLY

Let's load them all up and sail away. But that'd take a big boat. A really big boat.

GRACE

Must be one in an abandoned marina or shipyard somewhere. Adam could sail it.

SLY

That'd be exciting. Always wanted to be near the ocean. This'd be even better.

SFX. Sound of howling wind getting even stronger. Very intense storm.

GRACE

Sly, I've been wanting to ask you. You said your real name is Shu. You have Asian heritage, is that correct? Asian-American?

SLY

(Smiles) Yes, can't you tell. Mostly a mix of different Asian types, with a bit of other stuff thrown in, as far as I know. Why do you ask?

GRACE

Just curious. Thinking about what Adam has said about Tristan.

SLY

What about you?

GRACE

Mostly African-American, with Indian-American and Native-American, and other stuff thrown in, as far as I know. Just like you.

SLY

(They laugh.) What about Adam? Scottish?

GRACE

Yes, some, but mostly white meat for sure. *(They roar together.)* And Che is Hispanic-American. I guess the main thing is American.

SLY

You mean like the Tristanians? Mixed heritage but all Tristanians?

GRACE

Yes, but soon we'll all be Cascadians. Just Cascadians.

SLY

That's a wonderful thing to think about, Grace.

SFX*. Sudden rattling of the barn from howling wind brings them
back to present situation.*

GRACE

Wish they'd get here. Sounds really bad out there.

SLY

They may have passengers, don't forget. It'll take them longer.

GRACE

Is one of those horses a stallion?

SLY

Don't think so.

GRACE

Well, let's take stock. We need a billygoat, a stallion and a bull.

SLY

And a rooster and hen. That would be nice. And another cat.

GRACE

Don't like the cougar idea? What about pigs? A sow and a hog.

SLY

I don't like pigs! But I might have seen a couple somewhere.

GRACE

If we have pigs, we can leave the nice little lambs alone.

SLY

I love pigs.

GRACE

Thought you might. We'll need a huge ship, our own Adam's Ark.

SFX. Faint sound of horses plodding through the snowstorm.

SLY

Listen!

SFX. Long Pause. Stamping of feet of floor above.

GRACE

They're back.

SLY

No, wait. I didn't hear our signal.

GRACE

(Sotto Voce) Maybe he forgot.

SLY

(Sotto Voce) No, I don't think so. Something's wrong.

SFX. Someone attempting to come down. Movement of hay bale above.

GRACE

(Sotto Voce) Someone's coming.

SLY

(Sotto Voce) Uh, oh. Grab that shotgun. Outta sight. Kill the light. (She kills the candle.)*

Someone slides down tunnel. Lands with thump. Looks around.

VOICE

(Loud) Anyone here?

GRACE

You bet!

SLY

Look out. He's got a rifle.

He fires a rifle shot wildly. Grace fires shotgun. He falls to floor with heavy thump.

SLY

Good shot. You got 'im.

SFX. *Scuffle above. Shot fired. More scuffle. Falling body. Silence.*

GRACE

Something's going on.

SFX. *Morse code. Knock dah-di-dah. K for OK.*

SLY

It's him. It's Che. Our signal.

Sly returns knock in Morse dah-di-dah. Che slides down hay tunnel.

GRACE

Boy, are we glad to see you!

CHE

I hoped you'd be ready when you didn't hear our signal. Adam got the other one.

SLY

Other one?

CHE

As we headed toward the barn, they were waiting and ambushed us.

SLY

You're wounded.

CHE

Just a slight one. He got off one shot before Adam got him with the hay fork.

SLY

What are you smiling about?

CHE

I knew you'd be here to fix me up.

SLY

Don't be so sure. Three strikes and you're out.

GRACE

Where'd those two guys come from?

CHE

They must be friends of the others. Adam was right. We're not alone here.

ADAM

(Distant. Off.) Here she comes.

CHE

Hold on a second!

A young woman slides down very slowly and lands very hard.

CHE

Let me help you up. That was a hard landing.

SARAH

(Very softly) Thank you.

GRACE

It's a girl!

CHE

Her name's Sarah. She hasn't eaten for days. Milk's all gone. Do we have any more?

SLY

A little. Let me help you, Sarah. Warm up while I get some milk.

CHE

There's one more. Let's not forget Sam. She operated the radio transmitter.

SLY

Oh, yes! She?

Sam also slides down very slowly but lands lightly on the floor.

CHE

Samantha. Grace, can you help her? I need to help Adam.

GRACE

Can you take this dead guy with you? I hate looking at him.

CHE

He's not going anywhere. We'll get 'im in a minute.

Che crosses room and up tunnel.

GRACE

I'm Grace. This is Sly. Sarah has warm milk. We'll get you some.

SAM

Thank you. We're glad to meet you.

GRACE

Here's milk. We have stew as well. Get some bowls please, Sly.

SARAH

I'm starved.

Sarah slurps. Sly gets bowls, puts them on logs. Grace fills two.

GRACE

You'll warm up with this. Eat slowly or you'll get sick.

SFX. Signal K, then K by SLY.

Che enters. He holds three rifles, two new ones also high powered. Holds one up.

CHE
We have four of the finest rifles ever made. Night scopes. I found lots of ammunition in their saddlebags. Even some exploding shells. We're set. These guys must be part of their army.

Che notices Sam who holds one of the rifles with reverence. Adam enters.

CHE
You hold it as if you knew all about it?

SARAH
She does. Sam's been the top sharpshooter three years in a row.

ADAM
Pretty impressive.

SARAH
She can knock an apple off your head at a thousand yards.

SAM
Sarah's been second every time. She's also the rapid-fire champion.

CHE
What distance is that shot at?

SAM
She's hit ten out of ten targets at a thousand yards.

SARAH
Bigger targets.

CHE
Like the size of a man? *(She nods.)*

ADAM

(Holds up meat.) We've brought something tasty for the stew.

Sam and Sarah are slurping stew.

GRACE

What's that you're holding in your hand?

SLY

Pork? You killed a pig?

ADAM

Well, actually, a wild boar we saw in the brush. Che shot it and cleaned it.

CHE

And we have something else. We stopped at an abandoned barn. See these.

SLY

What are those? Chicken eggs? They're huge.

ADAM

Turkey eggs. Four of them. Didn't think they'd be missed.

GRACE

I've been craving eggs.

CHE

No, you can't eat them. We're gonna hatch them.

SLY

Baby turkeys? Bet they'll be cute.

ADAM

If all four survive that gives us seven chances out of eight.

SLY

Chances? What do you mean?

GRACE

He means to get at least one boy and one girl – to keep reproducing turkeys.

ADAM

That's not all. Show her the bag.

SLY

What's in there? It's moving. A snake? Uggh!

CHE

A rooster and a hen we found in the barn. They traveled well.

ADAM

Open it up. Let them out.

Che opens the bag. A hen emerges then a rooster.

CHE

And, we found that Border Collie. We call him Toby. He's with the two new horses. And Pandi. She moved over to keep them company.

GRACE

My word, you've been busy.

Howling wind.

SLY

Soon's this blizzard's over, can we move? Out of here?

CHE

Adam, we're just sitting pigeons. We gotta get outta here before someone comes.

ADAM

No one's coming here for some time.

CHE

Adam, you were wrong before about that. We were almost done for.

ADAM

Alright, so what do you want to do?

CHE

Move! They'll come back soon and we'll be trapped.

ADAM

If we move close by and they come back, then what?

CHE

We'll fight! Adam, we need to make a stand sooner or later. Why not now?

ADAM

(Long pause.) Alright, where do you want to move to?

Che doesn't have a ready answer to this but Sly jumps in.

SLY

When I was out there, I saw an old house far from the river, and a huge barn further away to keep all these animals, and a very lonely bull. And a couple of pigs. All we need now is a stallion.

CHE

Honey, look more closely at those two horses.

GRACE

Che's right. We should move all right. Far from here. Before we have more visitors.

SLY

Quiet. *(They freeze.)* I heard a noise. Like a voice calling out.

ADAM

It's the wind. Couldn't be anyone out in this storm. You imagined it.

SAM

I heard the voice too. Far away.

CHE

I've got to take the horses to the shed. Keep Bessy company, and our mare Mollie. I'll check on the voice.

SAM

I'll go with you. If it's alright. I'll take a rifle.

(He nods. She grabs one.)

CHE

Sure. Give me a hand with this guy. Now our cemetery'll have four.

They drag him into the tunnel and take him away.

ADAM

Notice how thin he is. They're starving. That makes them desperate.

GRACE

Sarah, how did all this start? What happened?

She takes the "pork" and begins to chop it up.

SARAH

We belonged to a community group that survived the plague. We lived on the coast one hundred miles south of the river. Sam and I grew up together. I'm seventeen, she's nineteen.

GRACE

I mean what made you go on the run?

SARAH

We get one day off a week. We saved ours to go on a long camping trip. As we were leaving, a big ship tried to land. It was chased by a small ship that fired on it then turned away. The other ship landed.

ADAM

A pirate ship? What did it look like?

SARAH

Sam can tell you better than I.

ADAM

What happened after that?

SARAH

The big ship carried the plague, but we didn't know it until we came back. They said "stay away until we fetch you". People were very sick. The commune was quarantined. No one in or out.

Sarah weeps. Sly consoles her.

SLY

Sarah, it's alright. Take your time.

SARAH

(Sarah pauses to control herself and finally continues.) We stayed away. No one came. We'd had little food. After two weeks we returned but everyone was dead or dying. We left.

GRACE

It must've been a really bad strain of one of the pandemic viruses.

SARAH

I guess so. We wandered north to the river. We went up river for twenty miles, found a boat and got across to the north shore.

GRACE

What did you do for food all this time?

SARAH

We ate roots and berries but got very weak. We're starved.

GRACE

Poor things. It must've seemed hopeless.

SARAH

Winter came. We were desperate. Sam found a transmitter and generator to call for help.

GRACE

Sam's quite resourceful.

SLY

And then what happened?

SARAH

When we heard from you, we started up the river but realized we knew nothing about you. We were afraid of being killed or captured.

SLY

Or worse. We understand.

GRACE

And you had no guns, or any way to defend yourselves.

SARAH

Then the snow came down hard so we holed up in a shed.

ADAM

It was amazing that we found them at all. We stopped in the shed and there they were. They were freezing and starving. Nearly dead.

SARAH

They came up with guns. We thought it was over, but they put them away, and Adam gave us milk.

ADAM

They drank every drop we had.

SARAH

(Sarah slurps.) Then we rode back through the snow, two to a horse.

SLY

The snow. Was it bad?

ADAM

Blinding. Bitter cold. Worse every hour.
SFX. Sounds of strong wind and snow blowing.

ADAM

We're in for one of the worst blizzards ever. Keep that fire going.

Adam starts radio, runs through frequencies.

GRACE

What are you doing now?

ADAM

Looking for other people. We need to increase the population.

SLY

We pioneer women know how to do that.

GRACE

After we finish eating, we'll show you. You don't need the radio.

*He stops. **SFX**. (B/G) Light static from radio as it's left on.*

Sam returns in a hurry without Che. She has Pandi and drops her.

SLY

You're back. With Pandi. Still snowing? Where's Che?

***SFX**. Wind and snow continue without abatement. Pandi hides.*

SAM

Up above. Adam, he wants you. Quickly.

ADAM

Something wrong?

SAM

Go. Hurry.

Adam leaves in a hurry up the tunnel.

SAM

You were right about the voice.

SLY

I thought so. Who was it?

SAM

Don't know. At first, we didn't see anything. A total whiteout.

SLY

Where was he?

SAM

We heard him a mile west. Down along the river.

SLY

How'd you know it was a person?

SAM

We took the horses north to the shed and when we got back here, we saw him. A scout.

GRACE

That's down near where the farmers used to live. What do you mean "a scout"?

SAM

He stopped calling. I watched through the scope. He looked around.

GRACE

Did he see you?

SAM

I doubt it but he did stare our way. Then Che sent me to get Adam.

SFX. Morse from Che and Adam. Sly responds. Che, Adam enter.

CHE

He didn't leave. Looks as if he has backup. Sam, Sarah, come with me.

He grabs rifles. He hands one to Sarah and one to Sam.

SAM

We'll need these.

CHE

We don't have much time. Sam, take the north side, Sarah the south.

SARAH

We'll split them up.

Che leads up the tunnel followed by Sarah, then Sam.

GRACE

Be careful. They probably outnumber you.

SFX. They split up: Sarah to south side barn. Sam to north. Distant rifle shot as they are seen. Four shots in rapid order at close range – south side, north, south and finally north. One distant shot is barely heard after first shot by Sarah. They return - Sarah, Sam, then Che.

CHE

I didn't get off a shot. They were awesome. That takes care of that.

ADAM

Not so fast. They lost four men, rifles and horses before. Now this. There'll be more.

CHE

When we were talking to Sam in Morse, they must have listened in to our plans, spotted us and followed us back. We're targeted. They won't give up. *(Roar of blizzard.)*

ADAM

I'm absolutely sure. They want to find us, take our food and kill us. This blizzard only stalls them so much. We've very little time.

CHE

What should we do?

ADAM

Che and Sam, move all the animals to that barn. Toby, our Border Collie, will help. It's a mile or so, so no one can hear noises from here. I'll harness Mollie to that wagon near the shed.

GRACE

What about the three of us?

ADAM

Collect all the food and supplies. Sly, help her if you can. Sarah, stand guard in case others come.

GRACE

What do we do with it?

ADAM

We'll move it to the big house. If we have time, we'll move two loads of hay for the animals.

GRACE

What about all the tracks? Won't they see them?

ADAM

If this blizzard lasts another day, the snow and wind will cover all the tracks. Questions?

SFX. Heavenly roar of blizzard continues.

SLY

What then? We'll find a big boat and sail away with all the animals?

ADAM

Yes, we'll find one. While you keep an eye out, Che, Sam and I'll head down river to that big marina on the south side. We'll look for a large schooner we can sail.

GRACE

And the rest of us?

ADAM

You'll work in shifts and hope Sarah won't need to test her rapid-fire skills. The house is about a thousand yards away. Toby will warn you if he hears any people. Could be many more coming here.

SARAH

If I see them first it'll take me ten seconds to get them.

GRACE

You can't go down this side. They'll be expecting you and you'll run into a trap.

ADAM

We have the advantage now. We'll ford the horses upstream, go down the south side and look for a schooner. I'll take the small boat so we can scout both sides at night.

GRACE

You don't know where they are. Won't you run into them?

ADAM

Even if we do, they won't be expecting us. When we sail down with the schooner, we'll never get past the mouth of the river and that pirate ship if we don't know where they are. We might have to take them out. Or maybe I should say Sam will.

SLY

How big is this schooner? We have lots of animals.

ADAM

One hundred fifty feet. Or more. Lots of cargo space below for animals and hay and the rest.

GRACE

Yes. Adam's Ark, we'll call it. He can sail anything. Can't you, Adam?

SFX. Radio crackling. Sounds become clear. Morse code is heard over radio. Dash dot dash dot, dash dash dot dash. CQ – Calling anyone. Over and over.

CHE

(Yells.) Adam, listen. It's the radio, the call signal. There's someone else out there!

SFX. HAL: CQ CQ CQ DE HAL SOS FUJI MM DOWN QTL N QUG HAL AR.

SFX. B/G. *Loose rigging, sails flapping, small engine stuttering.*

ADAM
It's a FUJI ketch. Mainmast is gone. Heading north. Forced to land. Sound of loose rigging, slapping sails, and the engine's in trouble.

SAM
A FUJI's thirty-five feet. Can't be too many people on board.

SFX. HAL: *CQ QTH S STR RIV CURR=NO FUL=NO FUD HAL AR.*

SFX. B/G. *Sound of engine dying, sails and rigging under duress.*

ADAM
The engine's dead. They're south of the strong river current. Out of fuel and food.

CHE
They're still calling with CQ. No one else has answered.

SAM
I know where they are. I was there.

SARAH
We should answer. You helped us. We should help them.

GRACE
Hold on a minute. Could be a trap. They could have the plague. Could be more of those pirates.

SLY
Or a couple of people like us. Take a chance. Answer them.

SFX. HAL: *SOS SOS SK. Radio sounds stop.*

ADAM
Too late. They're off the air.

CHE, SAM, SLY and SARAH
There's someone out there. We've got to go help them!

ADAM
Hold on. Something's wrong. Too much information. They don't want a response.

SARAH
What do they want then?

ADAM
Grace is right. It's a trap. Sam, tell me about that pirate ship.

SAM
There was a turret gun mounted on the bow.

ADAM
The ship itself. Length? Power boat or sailboat?

SAM
Thirty to forty feet long. Two masts, forward one taller.

ADAM
That was the pirate ship. They'll be on the north bank not the south.

GRACE
(Almost weeping.) There goes my island in the north.

ADAM
Doesn't change a thing. Now we know the location. Easy to find.

SLY
There're only three of you. What if there are 10 or 20 of them?

ADAM
I doubt it. They're starving and desperate. With Sam picking them off at 1000 yards, Che and I cutting off escape, we'll wipe them out.

SARAH
What about the pirate ship with the turret gun? The one Sam saw?

CHE

One exploding shell at the water line and it's sunk. I doubt they'll have time to launch.

ADAM

Everyone understand our plan?

GRACE

Yes, Captain. *(Others nod.)*

ADAM

After we finish down river, we'll bring the schooner up river, load it up and set sail north.

CHE

I'd love to mount a turret gun midships.

ADAM

It'd be in the way there but you can mount it on the bow.

GRACE

We can go to my island in the north? And have a nice safe home? *(Adam nods.)*

SLY

And we can take all the animals and have a real farm? *(He nods.)*

GRACE

(To Adam.) And you can grow vegetables and wheat and..

ADAM

And we can start raising a family. *(Grace looks at him and smiles.)*

GRACE

Where everyone is equal regardless of what they look like?

SLY

Including our children?

CHE

Just like how Adam described Tristanians?

ADAM

Yes. An utopian world rising from the ashes of the dystopian world that no longer exists. Wouldn't that be wonderful?

SLY

Where honor, decency, respect, and truth prevail.

GRACE

And hope, love, compassion, and caring.

ADAM

That's right. A new world. Well, let's get going. We have lots to do.

They each grab something. Adam exits first followed by Che.

SFX. *Grace hears a meow from the hay.*

GRACE

Sly, don't forget Pandi.

Sly goes behind some hay and returns cradling a frightened Pandi.

SLY

It's alright Pandi. We said all the animals. We can't forget you.

GRACE

(Softtly.) If we each have four girls, they each have four, and so forth, there'll be 30000 in 100 years. We pioneer women know how to be fruitful, and multiply, and replenish the earth.

Sly exits. Grace pauses at the exit before entering the exit tunnel.

GRACE

(Smiles.) Goodbye, burrow. You've given us warmth, nourishment, some safety, and maybe the start of a family. I won't miss the hay, but I'll miss you. *(She Exits.)*

End of Scene Two. End of Act Two. Curtain.

ENTR'ACTE

In front of curtain. Sly runs toward Che in the open and throws her arms around him. They are dressed warmly and wet from the torrential rain which has been falling. They talk loudly in the strong wind.

SLY
How did it go Che? Everyone alright?

CHE
Like a charm, just like we planned. We found the camp and quietly surrounded them. Adam and I started firing in a withering crossfire and then Sam started picking off the stragglers. Two guys headed for the ketch and the turret gun, but I hit the ketch at the water line and Sam picked off the two guys. I don't think there was anyone left.

SLY
It looks as if you found a schooner.

CHE
We'd found it before we went down to the camp and then came back and sailed it back up here. All this rain has raised the water level of this river so we are anchored closer to shore. Adam wants to load up as soon as possible and cast off. We already have a gangplank. What happened up here?

SLY
Nothing much until a few hours before you arrived. Four horsemen arrived heading for the barn. One had a torch. We didn't want to lose all that hay so Sarah started picking them off. She got the first two easily. The other two started to ride away. Sam got one but the last one rode toward some cover so she had to shoot the horse. Then she got the guy running on foot. She's an amazing shot. She felt badly about shooting the horse. We let the other horses free. What's next?

CHE
As soon as the rain lets up Adam wants to load up and sail away.

SLY
We'd better get going. *(They exit.)*

ACT THREE

Scene One: The curtain comes up slowly with the sounds of the horses and cow and bull and other animals muffled by the sound of wind, and the animals are below deck. It is dawn. The scene is toward the back of the schooner and includes the cockpit. Adam has the wheel and Che is off toward the bow, along with Sam.

SFX: (B/G) Soft muffled sound of rushing water nearby of the river rushing downstream, mixed with sound of wind racing across the open grassland, rustling reeds near river. Loud sound of Bubba the bull and Buck the stallion.

SAM (Off)
Gangplank is secure, Adam.

ADAM
Cast off, Che. Help him, Sam.

Che enters and crosses to stern and loosens rope.

CHE
Push off, Sam.

SAM (OFF)
Got it. Here we go.

CHE
(Removes rope.) We're free, Adam.

ADAM
Let's have a toast.

Grace, Sly, and Sarah join them in cockpit, bringing glasses with milk. Sam enters from bow. They raise glasses for a toast. Backdrop moves showing the boat drifting down the river. They watch the scenery drift by, then turn and wave toward the barn.

ALL
Goodbye old barn. *(They click glasses.)* Cheers! Bon voyage!

It starts to rain. Grace, Sly, and Sarah go below, and Sam to bow.

ADAM
Che, I wish we'd sailed together to the south. It's exciting to be on the open ocean. You'll love it.

CHE
Adam, you'll get your wish. We'll be on the open sea soon. You'll get enough excitement then. Meanwhile, I hope we get where we're going before next winter. I wouldn't want to be out at sea with a major storm. Especially not with this load.

ADAM
My plan is to hug the coast going north. Even with stops it should take no more than a couple of months. Maybe less. I've talked to Grace. We have a spot in mind that'll be perfect for our community.

CHE
First, we have to get this boat down the river and into the sea.

ADAM
No problem.

The boat is rocking slightly as they drift down the river. There are a variety of animal noises as the light fades. The light gradually comes up. Adam is at the cockpit showing signs of being very tired. Sam and Che enter from the direction of the bow.

CHE
Adam, be careful. Part of a fallen bridge is submerged. *(Points.)*

ADAM
I see it. *(Turns wheel.)*

SAM
Adam, why don't you take a break? Che can handle the helm.

CHE
Yes. We'll get you if we see some other fallen bridges.

ADAM

Alright, thanks. I could use a break. Watch out also for floating logs or submerged wrecks. This is a dangerous part of the river. And make sure someone is always on the bow watching for debris.

CHE

We'll be careful. Get some rest.

Che takes the wheel. Sam exits back to bow.

ADAM

With all those animals down there? *(Smiles. Exits below.)*

Grace enters from below. She looks at destruction on shore.

GRACE

(Calls down.) Sarah. Sly. Come up. *(They do.)* Look at that destruction. Incredible. *(They freeze with their jaws dropping.)*

SLY

I've seen some pretty bad things but this is the worst I've seen.

They watch in silence as they drift by scenes of warehouses and factories and other buildings along the river destroyed by fire, floods, wind, and looting, over a period of seven years.

SARAH

I didn't see anything like this on my way here. *(She goes below.)*

GRACE

Nor I. When I came from the north, I usually travelled away from cities and towns, like you, Sly.

SLY

Che, if we get a chance, we're going to have to stop and clean out the hold from the animal droppings.

CHE

There's a protected place on the south shore ahead. We'll stop there.

SLY

Good.

GRACE

We should be careful that a bridge doesn't fall on us while we sail under it.

CHE

As long as the wind is not strong, we are pretty safe. It has taken years to get to this state.

SLY

Seven years to be exact. *(She goes below.)*

GRACE

Call if you need help, Che.

She goes below. Sam enters from bow.

SAM

After we clean out the hold, I'd like to take a rest. Alright?

CHE

No problem. We all will. After we rest up for a day or two, Adam can take the helm and I'll handle the sails until we reach the mouth of the river. I hope that turret gun is still there on the ketch. I'd like to take it if it is. *(Slow fade.)*

There are sounds of animals as they are moved around and the hold is cleaned. There is a moment of silence and the lights come up with Adam at the helm. The view is of the destruction on the south bank. Che enters from the bow, and Sam from the hold.

SAM

The river is getting very wide. I don't remember this. We must have crossed upstream where it narrows.

CHE

I remember the mouth of the river as being very narrow. But there are deep bays on both sides of the mouth of the river before we get to the narrow opening.

ADAM

You are both right. It is several miles wide at the bridge, and beyond, west of it. Then there is a long spit that goes north, making a narrow opening to the sea where the current is quite strong as the river rushes out to sea.

The backdrop shows them drifting past Fort Astoria on the port side.

CHE

Look, Adam, is that the remains of an old abandoned fort? It looks as if it's a couple of hundred years old. The floods and tsunami have reached the base of the building.

ADAM

I think it's only a portion of the blockhouse they had here in the early 1800s, and probably a replica. All the other buildings here seem to be leveled or badly damages, so let's put the animals in there. *(Fade.)*

There are sounds of gangplank being put down, and animals being put ashore. Silence. Lights are dim showing all on deck. Dusk.

GRACE

(Comes from hold.) I'm glad that's done. All clean and sanitized.

The view is of open water as they cross to north shore.

SAM

There's the Fuji we shot up. *(Points off bow.)*

CHE

Adam, I want to recover that turret gun if I can. I left it intact.

ADAM

Alright, I'll sail alongside. Sam can help you.

Grace, Sly, and Sarah go below. Adam ties up stern. Che goes forward. Sam grabs a rifle and joins him.

CHE(OFF)

We have it. It looks as if it's in good shape. Where should we put it?

94

ADAM

Leave it on the bow. We'll install it later. *(Unties from stern.)*

SFX. Sound of a distant rifle shot. Adam ducks.

SAM(OFF)

Look out Che. Duck. It's two guys with rifles.

CHE(OFF)

I see them.

SFX. Sound of two shots nearby. Sam returns holding rifle.

SAM

Got them. Are you alright, Che?

CHE(OFF)

I'm alright. Let's get out of here before more show up. I thought we got all of them.

ADAM

It must be a group that is more widespread than I thought.

They sail out through the narrow opening of the mouth of the river. The scenes on port side show the sandy spit. Che returns to cockpit.

CHE

That's the sandy spit I reached coming up from the south.

SAM

Do you think that we'll see any ships at sea?

ADAM

We might.

CHE

We must expect it.

As they tack and sail north, the view on port is of the ocean waves.

ADAM

I want to reach a large bay I know about, before dawn arrives. We can stop there briefly. Watch out for rocks. *(Slow fade.)*

Signs of approaching dawn show Adam still at helm, with Sam joining him in the cockpit. Sarah comes up from hold with binos to join Sam. They are trying to spot an indentation while Adam tries to stay away from crashing on rocks. He tacks back and forth with the help of Che.

ADAM

Hard to port, Che.

CHE (OFF)

Got it Adam.

Sam spots the mouth of an inlet at the end of the long spit going north that they had been following.

SAM

Adam, it looks like the inlet you've been searching for, just beyond the end of the sandy spit.

Sarah spots a sign with her binos that had fallen to the ground.

SARAH

That sign on the ground says Willapa Bay.

ADAM

Coming about Che. Get ready to drop anchor, Che.

CHE (OFF)

Roger, you got it. *(Slow fade.)*

Late sunny afternoon. Grace, Sly, Sarah and Sam are snoozing on deck. Che and Adam take turns as sentries as well as preparing a wonderful meal. They bring it on deck. A gorgeous blazing sunset.

SAM

We call it Cascadia, Grace. What does that mean to you?

GRACE

(*Slowly.*) It means living a healthy and safe life and being able to do the things we always wanted to do. I want to write, to record everything I know about the Great Pandemic and our journey to get to Cascadia, and of course I want to have children, lots of them.

ADAM

I can help with that, especially the second goal.

Everyone laughs.

SAM

And what about you, Sly? What does Cascadia mean to you?

SLY

Well, I guess the same as Grace about finding a safe home where I can feel comfortable about having children and having them grow up learning things I never did. I also want to be on the sea and find oysters and clams and mussels and shrimp and crab and lobster.

CHE

I'll help you with that, Sly, and help make a wonderful soup with those ingredients for all of us, and especially to help eat it. Now that's what I call Cascadia.

They all laugh and agree.

SLY

When it's dark do you think we could let the animals out for the night?

ADAM

I think it would be alright. Let's do it. *(Slow fade.)*

Sounds of animals mooing and baaing and grunting and cackling. Then it is quiet. The lighting comes up dimly. Adam, Sam on deck.

SAM

When we passed that deep harbor some time ago, I thought I saw a sign that said Gray's Harbor.

ADAM

It was. We are making pretty good time but the wind is picking up.

Sounds of animals getting restless. Grace comes up. Boat rocking.

GRACE

Those look like ten-foot waves. These rough seas are disturbing the animals. Can't we put in somewhere?

ADAM

I don't think we have any choice since there is no harbor or bay. We must keep sailing until we find one.

Che enters from bow. He speaks softly.

CHE

Adam, this is too dangerous. We should turn back to that harbor. We won't lose too much time. It is better than capsizing with this load. We will lose everything, including our lives if we don't.

GRACE

He's right Adam. It's too risky.

ADAM

Alright. Let's come about Che. This also could be pretty risky.

CHE(OFF)

All set.

ADAM

Here we go.

Adam turns the wheel. Background shows schooner turning. Fade.

Che and Adam are on deck. Sam and Sarah come up from hold.

CHE

I'm glad we finally got that turret gun mounted on the bow. We've been lucky so far but I feel better in case we run into more pirates.

ADAM

I don't think we will. I'm more worried about rocks. I'm going to stay a mile offshore and sail without running lights. Sam and Sarah, would you keep an eye out for rocks or anything in the water?

SAM

Alright. I'll take first shift. Sarah can go below.

SARAH

How much farther do we have to go?

ADAM

I'd guess about one hundred twenty nautical miles. That should take us about four nights under best conditions.

CHE

The sky is pretty clear. The visibility is pretty high.

SAM

The twinkling stars above give off lots of light.

SARAH

What are those two things behind us? They look like ships.

CHE

They sure are. With this load we are slower than they are and they're gaining on us.

SAM

They're trying to cut us off.

ADAM

Alright Che. Time to test your turret gun. *(Che runs to bow.)* Ready?

CHE(OFF)

Alright Adam. Come about.

Ship comes about. Flash of light. Distant sound of small arms firing.

ADAM

Duck Che. *(They all duck.)*

Sound of loud firing of turret gun twice, followed by silence.

SAM

You got him.

SARAH

He's on fire.

SAM

What about the other one?

Adam tacks. Sound of loud firing of turret gun again. Grace and Sly come up, watch in silence.

SAM, SARAH, SLY and GRACE

You did it.

SARAH

He's sinking.

When things quiet down, Grace turns to Adam.

GRACE

Adam, we have a growing problem. We need to find a place to get these animals out for a little while. It is a mess down there and we can't keep up.

ADAM

Alright, I'll find a place. I think we'll find a spot a few hours north.

Slow fade. Sound of mooing and baaing and other animal sounds.

Lights come up with all six of them sitting around a splendid dinner spread out on deck. They are watching the sun set over the ocean producing a rich complex beautiful sunset of reds and oranges and yellows and pastel blues and pinks.

GRACE

Well, I'm glad that's done. What a lot of work. Time to relax.

ADAM

Are they all in?

CHE

Every single one of them. I kept track. Hope that's the last time.

SLY

That's such a beautiful sunset. I hope we have many more of those.

SAM

We never heard from Adam about his dreams and wishes. Well, Adam, what does Cascadia mean to you? What are you hoping for?

ADAM

Grace and Sly, remember our conversation about wine? Besides all the planting of crops, vegetables and fruit trees, I have wanted to make wine. Perhaps I can find some grape vines that are still viable and start the process of making wine.

GRACE

I remember that there were some vineyards on the island that we are going to, and also there was another really good winery that made excellent wine. It was on another island east of where we are going.

CHE

We will find them Adam. You can count on it.

ADAM

That would be one of the many things I will look forward to.

GRACE

And what about the cheese and bread to go with the wine? I can help with the bread but I don't know much about cheese.

CHE

I can help make cheese. I learned about that before the pandemic hit.

SLY

Don't forget Bessy. I like her milk but she will need to contribute some of her milk to make cheese.

SAM

We have goats now. I have heard that goat cheese is wonderful.

ADAM

That settles it. We are all in this together. We will finally get our wine and cheese and bread. Does that answer your question, Sam?

SAM

It sure does. I am looking forward to seeing how you make bread. I love fresh bread. Right out of the oven. I can't wait.

CHE

It won't be long. Meanwhile, I'm getting a little sleep.

Che got up off the deck. Slow fade.

Daybreak. They are anchored inside a bay sheltered from the strong winds. Adam is on deck in the cockpit. Grace comes up from below.

GRACE

Wow! That was some night. Rocking and rolling. It looks as if the wind is letting up. The place is a mess again. If Bubba and Buck get upset, they could smash the hold all to pieces. I'm doing all I can to feed them, keep them calm, and keep it a bit clean. Are you sure we are almost there? What's our plan?

ADAM

You described this end of the island once. We are almost there. It's just a matter of whether we take a shortcut through the pass, or sail all the way around the big island. Either way, we'll be docked by tonight and we can put all the animals ashore.

GRACE

I hope we can get through the pass. That storm we just survived is still out there.

ADAM

I sent Che and Sly to check out our chances.

GRACE

What about Sam and Sarah?

ADAM

They took the two horses onshore to scout the marina ahead. I gave them each a rifle just in case, and Toby went with them. He'll give warning of danger.

GRACE

Here comes Che.

Sound of rowboat pulled onto bow.

ADAM

Well, how did it go?

Che and Sly come back to cockpit with plumb lines in hand.

CHE

We don't think it's wise to try and enter the pass. The currents are tricky and rocks are everywhere. Furthermore, I feel, that with a draft of ten feet for the schooner, we will surely run aground and probably sink.

SLY

By the way it says Mosquito Pass and I was bitten by some.

ADAM

We'll have to go around the island as soon as the storm lets up.

CHE

What about Sam and Sarah?

ADAM

I sent them on horses while you were gone.

GRACE

Here they come. They're not alone.

SLY

It doesn't look as if they are in trouble. Those two guys are sitting in front. Sam and Sarah still hold rifles. And Toby has a friend.

GRACE

Well, I'll be damned!

SLY

And look, the one in front of Sarah is holding a cat.

ADAM

Tie the horses to a tree. Come aboard.

The four of them come aboard and sit in or around cockpit.

SAM

This is Ben.

SARAH

And this is Harry. And Toby's new friend is Sally.

HARRY

And this is Duke. He's shy.

Duke jumps down and goes into hold.

ADAM

We're glad to see other people, especially friendly ones. Welcome.

Adam, Grace, Che, and Sly shake hands with Ben and Harry.

GRACE

Where did you come from? We haven't seen a soul all this time.

BEN

Well, actually we live on another island nearby. We took a rowboat to the nearest island and found a small sloop to check out this island.

HARRY

We sailed on the sloop looking for supplies. We brought Duke and Sally with us. We've never left them alone before.

SLY

How have you survived so long when the pandemic decimated the population on these islands?

BEN

We did so by isolating ourselves.

HARRY

(He laughs.) If you knew our island, you would know this was not unusual. People generally keep to themselves so we just stayed there. We are pretty self-sufficient. We have a cow still and grow many vegetables and have chickens for eggs and meat. As you can see, we even have a cat to keep the rodent population down.

SAM

I hope Duke can charm Pandi.

BEN

Who's Pandi?

SAM

Our only cat. We could use more of them. Is there no one else left besides the two of you?

BEN

No. We have been considering leaving for some time and looking for others, but we have been concerned about running into diseases and wild people.

HARRY

But you do not look very wild.

SARAH

Looks are deceiving. We are actually pretty tough.

They all laughed.

BEN

Actually, we almost never leave our island. We picked a bad time. The storm hit us hard in the open strait just north of here. We paddled in to the protection of the marina. We barely made it.

SAM

And then we saw them walking on the road.

SARAH

They were afraid of us and our rifles so we put them down. And then Toby went up to greet Sally.

HARRY

We don't have guns. We don't like guns. We are peaceful people.

SARAH

So, then we brought them here.

ADAM

Well, you needn't worry. We are peace loving people as well.

GRACE

We call this Cascadia.

CHE

Adam, the storm has let up. Let's sail around the island while we can.

ADAM

Sam, would you and Ben ride the horses to the dock area and show us where the best place is to dock. Sarah, you and Harry can help us find the entrance without crashing into rocks or grounding.

GRACE

And then we can unload these animals for the last time. Here we come Cascadia. We are almost there. *(Slow fade.)*

Lights come up. It is dusk. They are all gathered together on deck watching the glorious sunset. A magnificent meal is laid out before them.

GRACE

Well, that's that. The animals are all safely offshore, fed, and happy. We are having our glorious last meal on board the Ark watching yet another spectacular sunset.

SARAH

Now Che, now that we finally got here, it's your turn to tell us your dreams and wishes about Cascadia. What do you want to do?

CHE

(He thinks for a moment.) I no longer want to build a guerrilla group, but we still need to be on guard. I want to live in peace, to have a family, to build a wonderful society where we all work together. I want to restore the good aspects of our old society. I feel sad about the loss of so many good people, good friends, but we need to look ahead now. I want to educate our many children that we will have. I also want to sail with Adam after we settle here and just explore the world. We will need to restore a few more ships. I am so excited about finally getting here and anxious to get started in the morning.

Everyone stands up and applauds Che for his fine speech, for he is often a man of few words, preferring action to talk. They watch the last glimmer of the sunset and turn in. Adam, Che, Sam, and Sarah take turns on deck keeping watch. Adam takes the first and stares at the dwindling light from the fading sunset. Lights out. Curtain.

End of play.

APPENDIX A: Author's Notes to Director and Actors

Although somewhat somber to start with, the mood of the play gradually changes. It should be played at a good fast pace from the start and by no means should it be "heavy". The sound effects about the weather are essential in creating the initial sense of isolation and helplessness. There is considerable humor which should be utilized to lighten the mood. The mood gradually changes until, in the final analysis, this becomes an uplifting and joyful play, full of hope and humor and love, and positive plans and community.

Act One, Scenes One and Two: In the initial scene each character is an individual focused on their own desires and goals and dreams. They coexist but are not together. This scene is filled with tension: the conflict between the two main characters, the threat and conflict with the immediate world just outside the "burrow", and the tension that comes from the huge uncertainty about the world at large. Adam, the provider/protector (hunter/gatherer) and versatile Renaissance man, is concerned about this. Grace (the writer/journalist/historian) is not. She seems oblivious to threats and possibilities in the outside world. They are joined by the two other members of this allegorical unit: Sly (the procreator) and Che (the warrior). As events unfold, by the end of the scene, they become a team, coalescing around the strong leadership of Adam.

Act Two, Scene One: In the beginning of the scene, as they learn about events outside, they are forced to abandon their dreams about joining a large thriving community, and become an even stronger team under Adam's leadership. They are all focused on the same common goals and they work together with a sense of purpose and a sense of future, and no longer with survival as the only goal. They no longer feel helpless. When contact with the outside world is made, this teamwork allows them to move into action. This scene should be played at a fast light pace with considerable humor. The underlying concern about Sly and the nature of her illness add some tension as the scene unfolds.

Scene Two: When new threats appear, their established teamwork serves to save them from disaster. They begin to plan for the future. They have become a very strong team, and finally feel hope and that their destiny is in their hands and theirs alone. When joined by two young starving people, they quickly assimilate them into their little group. In doing so, they learn of their unique talents which become essential as their plan unfolds. When additional contact with the outside world is made, as a team they are fully prepared to deal with it in confidence and hope. When an unexpected twist develops, they are also confident and resourceful, and resilient, enough to deal with this head on. As the play closes, they have jumped into action to convert their dreams and hopes into reality, regardless of the obstacles, knowing full well the significant hardships and challenges facing them. This scene should continue at a fast, upbeat pace and should be played with the greatest amount of humor and with joy and hope and love, and a strong sense of community.

APPENDIX B: SET DESIGN CONSIDERATIONS

The set described can be staged on a proscenium stage or easily done in the round, arena or thrust configurations. Staging in the round or arena style is particularly effective in creating the intimate atmosphere of the "Burrow". Creating good sound effects (SFX) and lighting are essential to the atmosphere in the burrow. Lighting with grids creating the look of hay is an example. Covering of blocks to simulate hay is another. Although the subject is somber, the acting should be with humor, and uplifting. Lighting should be between dim (1/2) and nearly dark, never bright.

In a proscenium staging, the audience (fourth wall) could be the back end of the barn (east) where there is activity looking out and moving of hay bales, but also at an angle to a side of the room with little external activity such as the north side or south (river) side. The entrance tunnel is implied to be opposite the back end of the barn and the escape hatch exit is implied to be near the back end of the barn.

In round or arena configurations no activity involving the outside should occur against the audience walls but rather in the corners, where some creative staging can be used for entrance tunnel, escape hatch exit and back end of barn where one can look out and light comes in. Use of one or more raised corners should be considered for round or arena staging. It's particularly challenging to have the sound effects in the proper location "outside" and above the stage. The same is true for lighting which comes primarily from outside the back end of the barn augmented with internal candle lighting.

For thrust configuration the open wall and the corners provide creative options for entrances and exits. Also, in the thrust stage, consideration should be given to a raised two or three-tiered stage.

In all configurations, the room created in the lower section of the barn, against the back of the barn, is implied to have hay on all sides stacked to the floor above separating the upper section from the lower. Entrance to this hay room is via a step tunnel that comes from high in the barn. The implication upon entry is of sliding down the tunnel then crawling into the room. The side of the room against the back end of the barn is implied to be one bale thick so that a bale can be removed to allow smoke out, air in, and to listen. The small (unseen) side room carved out can be on the north or south sides of the room or in a corner depending upon the locations of the tunnel entrance and escape exit.

APPENDIX C: PROP and SOUND COMMENTS

PROP LIST

ACT ONE, Scenes One and Two
Behind one bale at open
- Shotgun
- Binos
- First aid kit

Fire pit with grate/poker and pot on it (candle optional)
Two back packs
Logs to sit on
Chopping surface for kindling (axe) and vegetables (cutting knife)
Radio receiver
Milk and cups
Old writing paper
Sack brought in by Adam in beginning containing some veggies, and later in scene 3 by Che or Adam with "animals" inside.
High powered rifle brought in by Che at end of scene one and later in scene 3.

ACT TWO, Scene One
Morse code Transmitter
Generator and gas
Pail
Home made bowls
Pistol

Scene Two
Wild boar meat
Turkey eggs
Hen and rooster

SOUND EFFECTS

Rifle and shotgun Sounds
Radio Sounds and Morse Code Transmissions
Various animal sounds including hoofbeats
Weather sounds throughout (especially ACT Two)

CHARACTERS, HUMOR and COSTUMES

In the original version of this play, the characters in this play are ethnically neutral (ie. can be of any ethnic background), but this last version contains a few changes to allow a production to be ethnically diverse and to reflect the nature of a repopulated world. Early in the play, it is mentioned that DNA shows that mankind was descended from a small number of reproductive women 75000 years ago living in Africa, and the changes show the repopulation of the world along similar ethnically diverse lines. Casting should show that.

CHARACTERS

- Grace – Her knowledge of the world is exceeded only by Adam's. She has two roles: initially, as a self- proclaimed writer/historian, wanting to follow in the footsteps of Herodotus, Tacitus, Plutarch and Pliny, she is obsessed with the past and oblivious of danger. And yet we do see an unexpected flash of deep hatred and anger about how her life has been impacted. Coinciding with a first bit of humor in scene one, her "other" role of yearning for a safe home and family takes over. She becomes involved with their situation, and when necessary, becomes a "warrior" along with everyone else. Her cautious and negative attitude about the world outside seems at odds with the others but, in the final analysis, her words are heeded. She becomes an integral part of the "team" and no longer the lone voice. Grace is at least partly of African-American heritage, Indian-American, and Native-American.

- Adam – He is a very complex character as we discover, with a broad range of interests, knowledge and skills, covering agriculture, art, history and science. We first see him as an agricultural genius and the provider of food with his skills at pollination and propagation. We soon see another side of Adam, his obsession with the SETI like question of "Is anyone out there?" His many skills as radio operator (of Morse code) and general knowledge of science serve him well in pursuing this obsession relentlessly. Adam seems to have the answer to every situation and every challenge, and yet his naiveté and apparent passive nature causes Grace to push him relentlessly.

    When his dream, shared by the others, of joining a thriving community is shattered and events unfold, he becomes decisive and a man of action, and the unquestioned man in charge of the team. After a narrow escape and a final push from Grace, we see a new side of Adam as he assumes the full mantle of Commander in Chief.

Whether it is the realization of fatal danger approaching, the increased knowledge he gains, confiscation of high-tech weapons and good horses, or the arrival of two exceptionally skilled people that serve as a catalyst to catapult him into strong action, he becomes the strong aggressive leader the team has not seen before. Adam is of mixed ethnic background including largely Scottish.

- Sly – She is initially the clever fox or feral cat, seeking her own "burrow", her own nest or hole in the ground. She is a very sexual animal like the vixen seeking a mate with strong urges to procreate. Once she finds her mate and circumstances change, she turns her nurturing instincts toward animal husbandry and the salvation of many domestic species. Her positive upbeat nature and strong sense of humor are infectious and often carry the team through difficult times. Sly (real name Shu) is of Asian heritage.

- Che - He is the universal warrior, seeking a guerilla group to join, but, like the others, he must abandon that dream. He is fully prepared to take matters into his own hands and does at the end of scene one. Eventually, with the arrival of Sam and Sarah and their unique skills, which even he admires and envies, he becomes the leader of a small guerrilla team and the guerilla warrior he wanted to be, all under Adam's overall leadership. Che is of Hispanic heritage.

- Sarah and Sam - They surprise the team when their exceptional skills are revealed. They are warrior women (as exemplified by the Israeli women warriors in the early days of Israel as a nation). Their warrior skills come first as they are both an integral part of the "army". Their roles as procreators will come later. Each can be of any ethnic background, or racial heritage.

HUMOR
This is not a comedy but there is considerable humor throughout each scene, with each scene increasingly lighter and with slightly more humor. Often the humor is connected with transition points (character changes, entry of a new character). The second scene has much more humor than the first as would be expected with the lighter mood, and the third scene has even more, leading to a very positive, joyful, hopeful and humorous end.

COSTUMES
Costumes are described initially and suggested for Grace and Adam. Choice of costumes can add immensely to the atmosphere created in this underground burrow. They should be consistent with the lives each has been leading heretofore. They can also be a source of humor for the audience as part of lightening up the atmosphere. Thought might be given to the changing roles of the main characters as reflected subtly in costume changes.

APPENDIX E: DIRECTING/ACTING in ROUND

- Never stand or deliver dialogue in front of any of the four audience walls (pausing briefly in front of audience is OK or delivering dialogue while walking)

- Deliver dialogue from neck of four corners is key – almost all of audience can see

- Raise as many of four corners as possible
    - For example, the tunnel entrance in The Burrow can be and should be raised and concealed
    - The side room can be a step up raised area allowing dialogue to be delivered at a raised point (the neck)
    - Finally, the area which is later revealed to be the escape hatch should be raised allowing "escape" down thru raised area
    - All three raised corners are excellent for dialogue

- Dialogue in the center is most effective when one (eg., Grace in opening scene) is perched on a fixed raised corner (eg., east corner) and the other (Adam) is engaged in physical activity and movement and can take various positions during dialogue (Adam enters via tunnel –west, goes to side room – north, and then to fire pit – center east end, with lots of physical activity)

- General rule: stay low in center, stay high in corners

- Dialogue in center should be along diagonals so each person can be seen by half audience w/o blocking view – and as close to corner as possible to minimize blocking

- Dialogue with three or more should utilize same principles
    - Utilize strong points (corners, esp. raised corners) as much as possible
    - Utilize long diagonals staying close to corners
    - Stay low in center and maximize movement

- Avoid excessive movement in general (unmotivated crosses)